THIS BOOK IS FOR YOU IF.

- You have never cruised before and want an unofficial guide to cruising.
- You have cruised before and like the idea of reminiscing about your previous cruise(s).
- You have booked a cruise or holiday and want to get in the mood.
- You are time pressured and fancy a relatively short and uncomplicated read.
- You want to be transported into the world of cruising and imagine yourself sailing the seven seas.
- You want a feel-good factor read to raise a smile.
- You want a great holiday read or travel read.
- You love a good 'romance at sea' story.

ABOUT THE BOOK

Family Sailaway is the second in the Sailaway Trilogy and starts six months after the original book, *Surprise Sailaway.*

Sarah receives a flyer from CZN Cruises with some summer offers and makes plans for her next cruise. This time around, the cruise is longer, the ship bigger and there are more destinations to visit. Unlike the first time when she was with her younger sister, she has her aunt, uncle, cousin and boyfriend Paul, who she met on her first cruise, for company.

There are two other families on board who Sarah and the group will come into contact with, especially her cousin Megan who is young, attractive and single, but doesn't always get on with Sarah. Megan befriends another passenger, Rebecca, who says she is a cruise reporter but is acting very strangely. Sarah thinks she has seen her somewhere before!

Megan attracts the intentions of a married man who is with his wife, but likes the ladies too much, and a younger male passenger who is very shy and lives in the shadow of his younger, more confident brother. Who will win Megan's affections? How will it affect the other families?

A storm brews during the cruise which results in interesting scenarios and events for some of the passengers. Sarah's uncle Gavin runs an IT course, but due to the weather it has a direct effect on another family member.

Rebecca seems to know the Cruise Director, Craig. Is this just a professional relationship or is there something more behind the scenes? Sarah is curious and starts making her own investigations, dragging Paul along.

As the cruise sails back to Southampton, there are a few surprises in store. Sarah is closing in on Rebecca but is she on the right track? Will one of Megan's admirers be able to outfox the other? Will she be happy that he is the right one? Paul asks someone an important question, but will he be happy with the answer?

About the Author

Derek Curzon, whose first book *Surprise Sailaway* was released in 2015, now introduces his second book in a planned trilogy.

Born and raised in Dundee, Scotland, he studied accountancy before joining RBS in 1989. He has worked in accountancy, financial services and customer services.

Derek's first cruise was his honeymoon in 2005. After his fifth cruise in 2013, he decided to write about his experiences. This soon expanded to include characters, plots and his first book.

In 2012, he came second in a competition run by P&O to describe cruise experiences. He has written an article about cruising published in *50 Plus Magazine*. He writes a weekly, fictional cruise blog, *Nautical Nights*, which takes a humorous look at life aboard a cruise ship and the activities of the crew and passengers. Extracts can be found at the back of the book.

Dedication

To my wife, Sue, for her saint-like patience,
support and understanding.

ACKNOWLEDGEMENTS

Having decided to write the Sailaway Trilogy and particularly this book, *Family Sailaway*, there were two people who became a very important part of my team.

Chris Day, Director, Filament Publishing. Chris has provided a wealth of experience, guidance and knowledge along my publishing journey as a new author. His reassurance and assistance (and not always strictly in publishing) has enabled me to bring this book to fruition.

Wendy Yorke, Book Coach and Editor. Wendy has become, in a very short space of time, an invaluable colleague. Her professionalism and attention to detail have ensured that this book has been produced to a very high standard. It has been a pleasure working with Wendy and we have had much fun along the way.

Four's company – five's a crowd!

Family Sailaway

From the author of 'Surprise Sailaway'

Derek Curzon

Published by Filament Publishing Ltd
16 Croydon Road, Beddington, Croydon,
Surrey, CR0 4PA, United Kingdom
Telephone: +44 (0)20 8688 2598
www.filamentpublishing.com

ISBN 978-1-911425- 51-9
Printed by IngramSpark

Table of Contents

Bonus Feature: NAUTICAL NIGHTS

1 – NEW BEGINNINGS

"Come on, Hannah! We're going to be late!"

Hannah was scurrying around at the last minute again and her elder sister, Sarah, had seen this all before.

"I'm coming, Sarah," stressed Hannah.

"It would be good to arrive at our new apartment this side of midnight," Sarah said.

"Is she always like this?" asked Paul, who was helping the two sisters with their move today.

"Yes, but that's why I love her so much," Sarah replied.

It was late November, about six months after that wonderful, long weekend cruise, when Sarah and Hannah decided to sell the family home in Church Yarnton, a small village near Oxford, where they had found a new apartment.

The house seemed rather quiet and empty now, Sarah thought.

"Give me a minute, thanks," she said to Paul, as she went inside for one last time. Paul stayed in the small removal van he had arranged for the day.

Hannah came out of the kitchen and into the hallway where Sarah was now standing. They moved forward and gave each other a big hug. Hannah's emotions were getting the better of her and she started crying.

"Come on, Hannah," Sarah said in a soft, reassuring voice, "Let's have one final look round." Hannah nodded, but remained silent.

As the two sisters climbed the stairs together, Sarah's thoughts turned to those happy occasions in the past when they were growing up, firstly as children and later, as teenagers. They had only ever lived in this large detached house and it was a very happy and stable upbringing.

Since the very sudden death of their parents earlier in the year, however, their lives had changed forever and a move now seemed the best way forward.

Paul sounded the horn in the van, as they walked down the stairs.

"We really must be going now," he pleaded.

"Just a minute," Sarah shouted back.

The sisters walked round the ground floor for one last time. Sarah was picturing those numerous summer barbecues of yesteryear in the back garden and she could see her parents laughing and joking with their guests. She wiped a tear away and moved out of the house. Walking ahead of Hannah, she reached the van first and sat in the middle beside Paul with Hannah at the other side.

"All ready to go?" Paul asked.

Sarah looked towards Hannah, who just nodded.

"As ready as we'll ever be," Sarah said.

As they drove away, Sarah and Hannah looked behind for the last time. The house fell into the distance and their new journey from Church Yarnton to Oxford had begun.

Their apartment was a new development near the centre of Oxford, which was ideal for Sarah's work and Hannah's college studies. Spread across two floors, it was very modern and contemporary. Oxford was busy with Christmas shoppers, and by the time they arrived, it was becoming dark. The Christmas lights were on and everything looked rather festive.

Most of the bigger furniture had been moved earlier, leaving those last minute and smaller items on this final trip. Once everything was in the apartment, it was time for a drink.

"Where's the wine?" Sarah asked.

"It's in the fridge," replied Hannah.

"Well, it's not doing any good in there!" Sarah exclaimed.

Paul played 'mother' and poured them all a drink. They retreated to the living room, which together with the kitchen, bathroom and landing area, made up the ground floor. Two bedrooms and a second bathroom completed the first floor. After a bottle or two of wine were finished, they all fell asleep at various times, before Sarah awoke first.

Since their meeting on the cruise back in late May, Sarah's relationship with Paul was blossoming and she found herself in a very happy place for the first time in a long while. She collected the empty glasses, tiptoeing around not to disturb anyone and moved into the kitchen. Paul was awake soon after Sarah and followed her. They shared a kiss before laughing together.

"Shoo, you'll wake Hannah," whispered Sarah to Paul, but still laughing.

"She'll be fine. Anyway, I'm tired, aren't you?" he asked, rather seductively.

"Oh yes, not like you to be so forward, must be the wine," Sarah teased back. "I am tired, but not when Hannah's in residence!"

Paul was staying the night, but had to leave early in the morning and return to Milton Keynes. The two of them held hands while ascending the stairs, retiring for the night.

Hannah had been dosing for a bit and the muffled noises from the kitchen woke her up. Downstairs was in complete darkness as she walked across to the window. Like her sister, she had experienced a difficult year. The events immediately after the cruise hadn't helped one bit and she reflected on how they were changing her life more than she could have ever imagined.

2 – FAMILY HISTORY

Hannah was preparing tea when there was a knock at the door. After a moment, she opened it.

"Oh hello, it's Hannah, isn't it?" asked a middle-aged lady, rather hesitantly.

"Do I know you?" asked Hannah.

"Who is it?" shouted Sarah from inside the house.

Hannah didn't respond.

"You were at the funeral, weren't you? How did you know our parents?" Hannah asked the lady again.

By now, Sarah had reached the kitchen area and could see part of the lady standing outside. She moved closer behind Hannah.

"I knew your father many years ago," replied the lady.

There was an awkward silence.

"There's no easy way to say this, Hannah, but I'm your natural mother," the lady confirmed in a soft but quiet tone.

"Sorry, you're my what?" Hannah asked, rather dismissively.

"You had better come in," instructed Sarah to the lady at the door.

The three of them proceeded into the kitchen. The lady sat down first with Sarah. Hannah stood away from the table.

"You know about this, Sarah?" Hannah asked, because Sarah seemed very calm.

"I always had an idea, but it wasn't confirmed until about a month ago when I received a letter from Marion," Sarah responded.

'Wow, it's Marion, is it! We're on first name terms as well!" Hannah snapped.

"I can see this has come as a bit of a shock to you, Hannah," Marion added in a soft tone.

"You're not joking, given I seem to be the only one who didn't know what was going on. I'm assuming you're here to tell all, which certainly gives the last few days a sting in the tail." Hannah was in full flow now.

"Let's hear what Marion has got to say, Hannah. Does anyone want a drink?" Sarah asked, trying to defuse Hannah's obvious tension.

"Large gin, thanks!" bellowed Hannah.

"Strong coffee for me, thanks," added Marion.

Sarah started preparing Marion's coffee as she began her story.

"Your father, David, and I had known each other a long time, from school actually, but we went our separate ways afterwards. I stayed in the Oxford area and met your father by chance years later; after his marriage to your mother, Anne, and when Sarah was about five years old. We went for a few drinks and he explained that Anne couldn't have any more children, after complications with your sister, Sarah."

"Let me guess. You had an affair with my father, which meant nothing and the result was me?" Hannah barked, interrupting Marion.

"Hannah! Don't be so rude!" Sarah shouted at her younger sister.

"It's alright Sarah, this was never going to be easy," Marion replied. "David always wanted a second child and I think, on that particular night, one thing lead to another and in a moment of weakness, he spent the night. He said he regretted it afterwards and of course a couple of months later, I discovered I was pregnant," Marion continued.

There was another pause around the table. Sarah had sat back down after bringing the drinks. Hannah was still standing.

"How many times did you see my father at that time?" Hannah asked suddenly.

"Just a few times over a couple of months, I can't remember exactly how many now," Marion replied.

"Did you love him?"

"I had always liked your father and had known him a long time."

"Were you married at the time?"

"I never did marry, Hannah."

"Were you with anyone?"

"No, not at the time."

"Who decided I would live with Mum and Dad?"

We all did. Your parents and I decided it would be best, for you, if you were brought up by David and Anne, who was more than happy to raise you as her own."

Hannah turned her questions towards Sarah.

"You said Marion wrote to you about a month ago?"

"Yes, following her attendance at the funeral, she wanted to see you again."

"Did you reply to her?"

"No, I was going to wait until after the cruise we've just been on."

"So we're not actually sisters, only half-sisters?"

"I suppose we are, but you've always been my little sister and you always will be."

"Did our, your parents, ever speak to you about this?"

"No, but I'm sure they wanted to. Of course, it's too late now."

There was another brief pause. Hannah turned her attentions back towards Marion again.

"What are you after now, Marion?"

"After recent events, I was hoping the two of us could become closer."

"What do you think, Sarah?" Hannah turned toward her sister again. Her tone was, for the first time, slightly lighter. The initial shock had passed.

"I think some time for reflection might be best."

"But, you're not against me seeing Marion again?"

"It's not up to me, Hannah," Sarah replied in a soft tone.

"I think it might be best if I leave," Marion said. She rose from her chair.

"How did you get here? Where are you living now?" Hannah asked.

"By bus, and I live near Oxford," Marion replied.

"Leave a phone number, please. Just in case."

"I already have, in the letter, and I'm sure Sarah will let you see it."

"I'll see you to the door. Can we give you a lift home?" Sarah asked.

"No, thank you. I'll be fine, honestly," Marion replied with a smile as she reached the door. "Goodbye, Hannah. I hope we'll see each other soon?"

Hannah didn't respond as Sarah closed the door leaving them alone again.

"Well, it's not every day you meet your own mother after 17 years," Hannah said, turning towards Sarah.

"I wasn't sure how you were going to react, but I must say you handled it better than I thought."

"I think I would like to see her again, because it must have taken some courage for her to visit us today."

"I got that impression from her letter," Sarah continued. "I hope this doesn't change our sisterly relationship?" she asked nervously.

"Come here" whispered Hannah.

The sisters shared a hug and shed a tear again. It had been a long day for them and despite the revelations, Sarah and Hannah were very close and this wasn't going to change now.

3 – FESTIVE HOLIDAYS

Sarah was looking forward to Christmas. She was spending it with Paul and her favourite aunt and uncle, Louise and Gavin. They lived in Fort Augustus in the Scottish Highlands, and Louise ran a successful B&B business while Gavin was an IT manager for the Highland Council in Inverness. She hadn't seen them since the funeral back in February, and although the journey would be long, the holiday gave her the chance to catch up and introduce Paul to them both.

The drive north from Oxford took most of the day, but the expectation of a relaxed Christmas with family and each other's company kept them going. Tomorrow was Christmas Eve and they were here for four days, leaving before the New Year. After what seemed like an eternity, they were pulling up on the driveway. Gavin and Louise were waiting for them.

Sarah bounced out of the car and headed for Louise. They shared a hug together while shedding a silent tear.

Gavin headed towards Paul and, with a wry smile, started the introductions.

"You must be Paul, I'm Gavin, nice to meet you." They shook hands.

"And you," replied Paul.

"Woman, eh?" Gavin continued. "No emotional control."

"I heard that," Louise remarked.

"Only joking, dear," replied Gavin, backtracking slightly.

'So this is Paul. Well, let me see you two together?" Louise asked. Sarah walked back towards Paul, standing beside him.

"Oh yes, you look good together and happy," beamed Louise.

Sarah and Paul were going red, both embarrassed.

"Let's get these suitcases and you can settle in," interrupted Gavin, changing the subject tactfully.

Gavin and Paul brought the cases inside, while Louise and Sarah headed for the house.

"Although the B&B is closed, you'll stay in the spare bedroom next to ours, Sarah," confirmed Louise.

"That's great, thanks," Sarah replied.

Once the cases were brought in, Sarah and Paul declared how tired they were and went to bed soon afterwards. Gavin and Louise followed. There was going to be plenty of time over Christmas to catch up.

Hannah was not spending the Christmas holidays with them this year due to the events which happened straight after their first cruise and which changed Hannah's direction somewhat. She was spending Christmas with her natural mother, Marion, for the first time in her life. Her mother had fallen on hard times and was renting a one-bedroom flat in Oxford. However, they would be spending Christmas together in Sarah and Hannah's new apartment.

"I'm so glad you've given me the opportunity to spend some time with you, Hannah," Marion had said.

"Not at all, I'm happy you came that evening otherwise we wouldn't be sitting here now," Hannah concluded.

Louise was up early the following morning and although her business was closed, the routine was hard to stop. Gavin followed soon afterwards.

'Don't they look good together?" Louise asked.

"Yes, they do, but calm down, we don't know much about Paul yet."

"All in good time!" replied Louise.

"Talking of not knowing much, what do we actually know about

Marion? My sister Anne never did tell me anything about 'the other women' all those years back. I wonder how she really felt about her husband's affair?"

"Only the basics we've been told from Sarah, but it's not really our business or place to press. I'm sure Anne would have forgiven her husband; she was that kind of person."

"I suppose so. Although it's a pity Hannah couldn't make it up here to see us," Gavin said.

"Yes, but I'm sure Sarah and Paul will more than make up for it."

It was lunchtime before Sarah and Paul surfaced. After a snack lunch, the four of them took a walk round the village and along the canal. A table for four was booked later for an evening meal together. At the restaurant later, the atmosphere was festive and expectant. The party soon split into twos, with Louise quizzing Sarah about Paul, and Gavin and Paul talking work. Gavin changed the subject.

"Have you ever sampled a malt, Paul?"

"No, I don't think I've had the pleasure," Paul replied.

"We'll have to change that!" Gavin beamed.

"Now don't be leading the poor man astray, Gavin," said Louise but with a tone Gavin had heard before. He knew he would be in trouble later!

"One or two, dear, just for the road," Gavin continued.

"Can you recommend anything, Gavin?" Paul asked politely.

"I have just the one, wait here a minute. Anyone else?" Gavin asked, now smiling.

"Go on then," confirmed Louise for her and Sarah.

After a while, Gavin came back with four malts.

"Now, you have to drink this in one," instructed Gavin.

"No, you don't!" confirmed Louise, looking at Paul.

Despite Louise's warning, they all obliged. Paul was taken by surprise and started coughing and spluttering.

"Welcome to the family!" shouted Gavin.

"Gavin, I warned you!" barked Louise.

By this time, Paul had stopped coughing and had regained himself.

"Are you alright?" asked Sarah reassuringly.

"I'm fine, but revenge will be sweet," confirmed Paul.

"Excellent, that stuff is enough to clear any cobwebs," Gavin continued, now glancing at Louise for approval.

"Well, if everyone's finished, I think home is calling," Louise stated, rising to leave the table. Sarah followed with Paul behind.

"Oops, the boss has spoken," whispered Gavin to Paul as they left the table.

Christmas Day was a very relaxed affair. Louise was up early preparing the festive lunch and was joined by Sarah. Gavin and Paul went out for a walk and returned later. Presents were exchanged, TV programmes watched in the afternoon, and drinks enjoyed all round.

It was early evening when Sarah decided it was time to phone Hannah and wish her a Merry Christmas. The conversation they had was pleasant with lots of laughter. Both sisters were relaxed and happy in their respective company. The events of that night six months ago hadn't drawn them apart. If anything, they had brought them even closer together.

"Everything OK with Hannah?" Louise asked.

"Yes, it sounds as if they are having some good catch-up time together."

"It's a pity she couldn't be here," Louise was fishing somewhat.

"There will be other times, I'm sure."

Later that evening, remembering the games Sarah and her family had played here before on those evenings while they were touring the Highlands, Sarah made a suggestion.

"Blackjack anyone?"

"Excellent idea, Sarah! Who wants to be dealer?" Louise asked.

"I don't really understand the game, so I will," Paul volunteered, now looking at Gavin with a chance of revenge looming.

After a brief confirmation of the rules, the game was underway. Paul was growing in confidence with every passing hand and, with the drink kicking in, was playing a blinder, limiting the other three players to sporadic wins. Gavin was becoming increasingly frustrated with his lack of success.

"Revenge is sweet, I think. Is this the best you can do, Gavin?" Paul was in full swing. "Have you any malts for me to try here, Gavin?"

Paul and Sarah high-fived.

"You've been rumbled, Gavin. Come on, serve the man his malt!" Louise exclaimed.

"Welcome to Scotland, Paul!" Gavin confirmed, pouring him a malt.

It had been a very enjoyable day, Sarah thought, and there was better to come tomorrow, she hoped.

Sarah and Hannah had received a flyer from CZN Cruises last month and, as previous passengers with them, they were offering discounts on selected cruises on their flagship liner, *The Atlantic*. Sarah had patiently waited until after Christmas to introduce the idea of a cruise to her aunt and uncle. Boxing Day now seemed the right time.

"Paul and I are thinking about going on a cruise next year," she said.

"Oh, that's nice, where to?" asked Louise.

"Well, we're not sure yet, but following our cruise in May, we've received some discounted offers for next year. Have the two of you ever fancied a cruise?" Sarah was 'fishing' for information now.

"Not really given it much thought to be honest," replied Gavin. "I mean, what do you do on a cruise?"

"Have you something in mind?" Louise jumped in.

"Oh, there's loads going on aboard a cruise ship these days. I know Hannah and I thoroughly enjoyed our first cruise and, of course, that's how Paul and I met, so it can't be that bad," confirmed Sarah. "We were thinking about the possibility of the two of you joining us next year and benefitting from these offers."

"You've brought some details with you?" Louise asked, again almost anticipating the response.

"Funny you should mention that because we have," Sarah confirmed.

"Let's have a look," Gavin sounded as if he was becoming more intrigued. "Isn't it primarily for a more elderly clientele?" he continued.

"I think it used to be, but not now. They seem to be attracting more families and younger couples. You'll fit right in," Sarah continued in full flow.

"Cheeky, we're only in our early fifties," barked Gavin.

"Exactly, what we were saying, fit right in," Paul backed up Sarah's previous remark.

After the initial browse of the flyer, websites were out and comparisons made. Gavin and Louise were warming to the idea.

"What do you think, Gavin?" asked Louise.

"It would certainly be a first for us, but why not?" he confirmed.

"My sister can run this place while we are away. How long would the cruise be for?" quizzed Louise.

"The one we're looking at is for a week in July," Sarah confirmed.

"That should be alright, my sister owes me a favour anyway," Louise said, now smiling.

"Booking for four?" Paul asked hesitantly.

"I'm assuming Hannah is alright with this?" Louise asked.

"Yes, she's fine. I think given the choice, she'll spend as much time as she can with Marion."

Louise and Gavin nodded in agreement, looking back at Paul.

"Great, I'll book it when we get back to Oxford. You won't regret it, I promise," Sarah continued.

Having spent Christmas Day at her apartment, Hannah and Marion spent a couple of days at her mother's flat. Marion worked part-time and although her flat was small and cramped, it was clean and tidy. The sale of the family home had provided Sarah and Hannah with additional savings after buying their apartment. Having spent some time with Marion in her flat, Hannah had a proposal.

"I would like to help you buy or rent something better," she said.

"You don't have to do that, Hannah."

"I know, but I would like to. What notice are you on here?"

"Just a month, I think."

"In the New Year, we'll go house hunting!"

"I can't really afford anything bigger."

"But I can, so that's settled it."

Sarah had hoped the suggestion of a cruise for the four of them would be too good an opportunity to miss for her aunt and uncle and in the end, she didn't have to persuade them too hard. She had always enjoyed their company over the years and was sure next year's cruise would be very enjoyable for them all. When they were ready to leave Fort Augustus very early in the morning, they were reminded to book the cruise as soon as they arrived home and to confirm it with them.

"We'll speak soon," Sarah shouted as the car drove away.

Gavin and Louise waved them off. The journey south was dominated with cruise talk and how great it was going to be for the four of them. When they arrived back at Oxford, it had been a long day and Sarah and Paul were tired. Paul was staying an extra day before he had to drive back home. Hannah was away staying with friends now and they had the place to themselves. The following day was relaxed and quiet.

"Remember the last time you said not if Hannah was in residence?" Paul teased slightly.

"Yes, I remember and of course she isn't. In residence, I mean," Sarah replied.

Sarah and Paul's relationship was more than blossoming and Sarah's bed hadn't been christened yet since they had moved in last month. Tonight, however, was to change all that. It was going to be another 'early' night.

4 – FOUR'S COMPANY, FIVE'S A CROWD

Megan was having a bad year. Her parents were in the middle of a messy divorce and she was halfway through studying towards an economics degree in London, where she currently lived. It had been agreed that during the summer, she would spend most of the time with her aunt and uncle in Fort Augustus.

To save journey time, she booked a flight from London to Inverness and because Gavin worked there, it was a short trip for him to the airport to collect her. Megan was anticipating a relaxed holiday, but she was going to be helping out at Louise's B&B. Megan left a rather dreary day in London and on arrival at Inverness, the sun was out on a beautiful June's summer day.

"Welcome to sunny Scotland, Megan," Gavin beamed.

Megan rarely visited this far north and had only been to the B&B once before.

'Wow, the sun does actually come out here," she teased. "In fairness, it was raining when I left London earlier."

Gavin just ignored the comment. "Pleasant trip?" he enquired.

"Yes, thanks, and looking forward to a holiday now," Megan said with a smile.

Gavin was going to comment, but thought it better to leave it to Louise to explain Megan's 'holiday'!

Gavin and Megan were soon back at the B&B. As with Sarah and Paul's visit, Louise was there to greet Megan. Gavin and Louise didn't have any children themselves and treated all their nieces the same, always enjoying their company when the situation arose. Megan, like Sarah, had a business mindset and always had a good banter with her aunt and uncle. Her parent's marital situation made no difference to Gavin and Louise's affections towards her.

There was the obligatory family hug between Megan and Louise while Gavin brought Megan's things in.

"You've brought the good weather with you, I see," beamed Louise.

"Yes, I was just saying the same to Gavin," she confirmed. "I'm looking forward to a holiday, now I'm away from that mad house,"

There was a pause. "You do know you're here to give me a hand though?" Louise asked slightly surprised.

"Oh yes, but there's not much to rustling up a few bacon rashers and making a couple of beds in the morning," sounded Megan in all sincerity.

"Whoops, wrong thing to say, Megan," whispered Gavin.

"I'm going to assume you're joking!" Louise remarked.

"Yes, joking, Aunt," Megan back tracked, looking sheepishly towards Gavin.

"Oh, I can't save you now."

"Anyway, I brought you this as a thank you for having me for the summer," Megan quickly changed the subject.

"Oh, you didn't have to, silly," Louise said with a softer tone.

"What is it?" Gavin asked reaching across to look. "Oh forgiven immediately, it's a bottle of malt whisky!" beamed Gavin, now studying it intensely.

"Well, you've made someone's day anyway," confirmed Louise. Now tomorrow I'm not expecting you to do anything. You've had a long journey today, so I think we can break you in gently."

"Yeah, that's fine, thank you. I'll see what Fort Augustus has to offer."

When Megan had gone to bed, Gavin and Louise talked about next month's cruise.

"We'll need to mention this to Megan tomorrow. I just hope she decides to come with us and join Sarah and Paul," Louise stated, feeling rather concerned.

"If she doesn't want to, she can stay here and help your sister. I know the two cousins don't really get on and as for the other 'issue', we can't do anything about that until we speak tomorrow," confirmed Gavin.

"Tomorrow it is then," and with that, Gavin and Louise retired to prepare for their guests in the morning.

With the guests for the day having left and Gavin gone to work, it was time for Louise to introduce their forthcoming cruise into the conversation.

"You know this cruise the four of us are going on next month, Megan," Louise started hesitantly.

"Yes, I know Hannah mentioned it to me earlier in the year. You're going for a week, aren't you?" confirmed Megan.

"That's right, we are, but Gavin and I were thinking, hoping, that you might want to join us aboard?" Louise continued a little nervously.

"I could certainly do with a holiday, now that I'm working here, but I don't know if a cruise is my thing really. Too many elderly people and what do you do on a cruise anyway?"

That last comment gave Louise the chance to fast forward the conversation.

"Well, that's what we thought when Sarah and Paul first mentioned the idea, but when we looked into it, it really does look promising and there's loads to do on board. Apparently, the ship is brand new this year and I'm sure a bit of relaxation and sunshine won't do you any harm," Louise continued, now on autopilot.

"Wow, when did you become a spokesperson for the cruise industry?" asked Megan teasingly.

"Yeah, it sounded good, didn't it? So what do you say?" asked Louise, now striking while the iron was hot.

"I suppose it wouldn't do any harm but I'm not doing a Sarah and looking for holiday romances," Megan confirmed.

"Everyone's different, Megan, and I'm sure your cousin didn't actively hunt Paul down, but that's great you're going to come along. All you need to bring with you is some spending money because the cruise itself is our treat and, of course, some summer clothes, and you'll be fine."

"You've already booked my cabin, haven't you?" quizzed Megan.

"There weren't many cabins left, so you have an inside cabin, I'm afraid," added Louise, avoiding Megan's question.

"That doesn't bother me not seeing the sea because I don't think I travel well anyway."

"Good, I know your uncle will be as pleased as me that you're coming with us. You'll also be able to meet Paul, he's very nice."

Louise couldn't wait to tell Gavin the good news when he arrived home. They had indeed gambled slightly on Megan saying yes to the cruise, but her agreement to come ended any problems this might have created.

Megan was warming to the idea having studied the website and brochures. Although, in a family group of five, she was free to do what she pleased, within reason, and could actually have a stress-free and relaxing time, a million miles from the troubles and studies back in London. A cruise was just what Megan needed right now, she thought.

5 – MAIDEN SEASON

CZN Cruises were a small cruise operator with a handful of ships and limited itineraries. However, they were an efficiently run, family business that had attracted the attention of a few large-scale USA operators. One of them had already made an offer for the company, which had been rejected. Another reason for the attention was CZN's new flagship liner, *The Atlantic*, which carried 3,500 passengers with more than 1,000 crew. Making its maiden season, it was going to extend the company's itineraries and make it a major player in the UK and European market. On exchange days in Southampton, it dominated the skyline with its blue and yellow funnels and gleaming white exterior.

Craig, the Cruise Director, had a problem. He was responsible for the day-to-day entertainment aboard the Atlantic but an IT lecturer, who was going to give two teaching classes on board, had suddenly become ill and could not make the cruise. Craig had an idea.

"Sharon, have we sent the *News* out to passenger's cabins yet?"

"No, but it's due out very shortly," she replied.

The Atlantic News was the passenger's daily events magazine, which let them know what was happening on the ship each day.

"Right, add this short paragraph to the bottom of the back page, will you, please?" Craig continued. "'Due to unforeseen circumstances, we are looking for any passengers with IT experience who would like to take two classes during the cruise, teaching the basics to other passengers. Please give your details to reception tonight.'"

"I'm not sure how much response we'll get for this. It's very short notice," Sharon replied.

"Let's see, you never know. As my gran used to say, it only takes one."

Gavin, Louise and Megan travelled down from Fort William and stayed overnight near Birmingham, before meeting up with Sarah and Paul the following day near Oxford. The five of them travelled down in two cars. Megan's car was first to see the ship, which was shining bright in the July sunshine.

"That's an impressive-looking ship. Our floating hotel awaits us." said Louise. "Funny to think that Sarah and Paul met on one of these ships last year."

"Holiday romances are not really my thing," Megan replied. "I am looking forward to the sunshine and a relaxing week though."

Gavin, who was driving, didn't have the opportunity to view the ship as he parked up in turn instructed by the liner staff. Although early afternoon, the whole place was a hive of activity and soon the three of them were making their way to the terminal. Sarah and Paul arrived a few minutes later.

"Who would have thought when we boarded that cruise last year that our next one would be all together," commented Sarah.

"It just goes to show, you never know what is round the corner," replied Paul.

After a small wait at check-in, the five of them met up in the lounge area. A new terminal building had recently opened and, given the increased number of passengers now sailing together, the lounge was used to hold passengers until they boarded. As the party were now together, Sarah started the introductions.

"Megan, I'd like you to meet Paul, Paul, this is my cousin, Megan." Megan and Paul shared a friendly embrace.

"So you're the Paul Hannah keeps talking to me about. You want to be careful, Sarah!" teased Megan.

Paul started to go slightly red in the face.

"Oh, I don't need to be careful, thanks, Megan. I know Paul's not Hannah's type!" replied Sarah in a firm tone.

"So now we're all here, shall we find some seats together?" asked Louise, diverting the conversation.

They moved to a quieter part of the lounge where there were unoccupied seats. The lounge was filling quickly as more passengers streamed in. An announcement came across the tannoy to confirm boarding would start shortly and at the same time, a couple who seemed quite agitated walked across the lounge towards them.

"I thought you said you had them?" shouted the man.

"No, I'm sure you said you collected them after we passed through security?" replied the woman.

Louise smiled gently towards the woman but said nothing. The woman continued. "Ah, I've found our boarding passes, but you must have placed them here yourself!" she confirmed.

The couple moved away towards the refreshment area, still arguing.

"Wow, is that what married life does to you?" commented Sarah, noticing both the wedding rings the couple wore. "I thought a cruise was supposed to be a relaxing affair?"

"Who says they're married to each other?" quizzed Megan.

"Megan?" Louise smiled.

"Just saying, never want to assume."

"This is when we never enter the conversation," whispered Gavin to Paul. Paul nodded in response.

"Who's betting that couple's cabin is in between ours?" asked Louise looking at the others.

"You're joking, aren't you? Do you know how many cabins there are on board this ship?" replied Paul in disbelief.

"What's the bet then, a bottle of champagne?" Louise continued.

"Oh happy days, this is easy, you're on!" replied Paul. "None of the cheap house plonk either, you understand!"

"You're on, and we have plenty of witnesses," confirmed Louise, still feeling confident.

Another tannoy announcement confirmed passengers could start boarding, depending on the coloured cards they were given on entering the lounge. Sarah and party were soon ascending the ramps towards the ship. As they turned a corner, there was a small queue of passengers waiting their turns to board. There was a gap behind them but they could hear approaching voices.

"I've a feeling I recognise those voices," said Gavin with an air of inevitability.

Just then, a familiar couple turned the corner and stood just down from them all. It was the arguing couple from earlier.

Louise smiled to the woman again, but this time introduced herself.

"I'm Louise," she said.

"Oh, it's Helen," she replied, somewhat taken aback but very relieved. "This is my husband, Neil."

"Isn't it a grand ship?" Louise continued her ice-breaking.

"Yes, it is," Helen replied.

Neil and Gavin exchanged a quick glance in acknowledgement before Neil shared a longer look with Megan.

Helen and Neil had been married three years and this cruise could be described as a 'make-or-break' holiday for them both. In their late twenties, Neil was two years younger than Helen, but hadn't really settled into married life. Helen was a nurse, Neil a policeman and with shift work including nights, their work patterns added to the challenges in their marriage. After a short while, Sarah and her family group were boarding the ship for the first time.

"Wow, this is much bigger than the ship we were on last year, Paul," gasped Sarah.

"Yes, and I remember getting lost last time trying to find my cabin. I'll let someone else have a go this time."

"Good afternoon, sir, madam, and welcome on board," said an officer.

Other crew members were on hand to guide passengers to their cabins. They were soon at the lifts ready to take them up the decks. Megan was out first because her inside cabin was only a couple of decks above the main atrium area where they had boarded.

"I'll come and check on you later," Louise confirmed.

"That's fine, thanks," replied Megan as she exited the lift and made her way towards the corridor.

As Megan made her way towards her cabin, she could feel the presence of someone behind her. She turned around to face another woman of a slightly older age walking towards her.

"Do you know where my cabin is?" said the woman showing Megan her cabin number.

"Oh, you must be just along from me, on the same side," confirmed Megan.

"Thank you very much," said the woman. "I'm Rebecca. Are you travelling alone as well?" she asked.

"No, some other family members have cabins further up the ship. I'm Megan, by the way."

Rebecca just smiled.

"Have you been put in the naughty corner?" Rebecca quizzed, now teasing slightly.

"Not really, anyway I hope you enjoy your cruise," Megan answered, changing the subject.

Rebecca squeezed past Megan and walked along the corridor. Megan opened her cabin door to reveal a very tidy, if not rather small, cabin. However, it had all the essentials, including no sea view, which she was happy about; TV; en-suite with shower; and enough cupboard space for all her clothes. Her suitcase was waiting for her on the bed and she quickly started to unpack.

Sarah and her group found their cabins and when they entered, Sarah and Paul's luggage had arrived, but Louise and Gavin's hadn't.

"I'm going to check if Sarah and Paul's luggage has arrived," confirmed Louise.

As Louise exited her cabin, two familiar faces came walking towards her.

"Are you lost?" asked Louise, now looking at Helen and Neil.

"We were, but I think our cabin is here," Helen said, relieved to have found it.

"You're in this cabin?" said Louise, leaning on the door.

"Yes, I think this is the one," confirmed Helen.

"Well of all the cabins, wait until I tell the others!" beamed Louise.

"Have we missed something?" quizzed Neil.

"Not really, but I think I've just won a bottle of champagne!" Louise continued, still smiling.

Louise, now distracted, went back to her cabin to tell Gavin the good news.

Sarah and Paul had started their unpacking.

"I'm going to check on Megan," confirmed Sarah.

"I thought Louise said she would do that," Paul replied.

"I won't be long," Sarah replied as she exited their cabin.

Sarah made her way down the stairs to where Megan's cabin was. After a short walk along the connecting corridor, she knocked on Megan's door. The door opened.

"Oh, it's you, I was expecting Louise," said Megan despondently.

Sarah moved inside towards a chair in the corner. Megan had always been closer to Sarah's sister, Hannah. Both were of a similar age and they had often socialised together over the years. This cruise was Sarah and Megan's first meeting since the funeral almost eighteen months ago. Sarah had never really forgiven Megan for leaving Hannah in the state she did after the funeral.

"I thought I would check to see if you were settling in OK," Sarah said, now standing near the chair.

"I'm fine thanks, but I'm sure you could have found that out from Louise. Where is she anyway?"

"I didn't like how you left Hannah at the funeral," Sarah continued, ignoring the question.

"We were having a laugh together and it probably helped Hannah to get through the day," Megan answered back.

There was a moment of silence.

"It's not going to spoil this week's cruise, though?" Sarah asked.

"No, not from me and anyway, I'm looking forward to a week of sun and relaxation," Megan replied.

Sarah moved towards the door.

"Right, I'll see you later then?" Sarah confirmed as she opened the door.

Megan smiled back but didn't reply.

Louise opened her cabin door and, with a beaming smile, approached Gavin inside.

"You're not going to believe who's in our neighbouring cabin?"

"No, but I've a feeling you're going to tell me and I'm not going to like it!" Gavin replied.

"Only Helen and Neil who we met twice earlier! I saw them coming along the corridor just now!"

The conversation was interrupted by raised voices in the next cabin.

"I see they haven't finished the argument from earlier," Gavin said dismissively.

"I'm going to invite them to join us for drinks after our meal tonight," confirmed Louise. "It might do them good to be in larger company," she continued.

"Of course you're joking, I mean they probably need or want to be alone?" Gavin asked despairingly.

Gavin looked across at Louise and realised quickly she wasn't joking. He just sighed.

"I like Helen and she looks like she could do with some moral support," Louise concluded. "I'll go and ask them now."

"Right, I'm going to check on Sarah and Paul to see if their luggage has arrived, which I recall you were going to do," Gavin said more firmly.

Gavin left the cabin first and made his way to Paul and Sarah's cabin. He knocked on the door and was greeted by Paul.

"Has your luggage arrived?" Gavin asked.

"Yes, I'm nearly finished unpacking."

"Ours hasn't. I think I'll take a walk to reception. Sarah not with you?" Gavin asked again.

"She went to check on Megan even though she hadn't finished with the suitcase. I did ask, but I was ignored," confirmed Paul. "Can I come with you?" he asked.

"I know what you mean about being ignored," Gavin replied. "Yes, of course. Come on, we'll go down now."

Gavin and Paul made their way down to the reception via the lift and across part of the atrium. The ship was starting to fill now and there was a small queue when they arrived. However, it wasn't long before a member of reception soon addressed them.

"Can I help you, sir?" she asked.

"We haven't received our luggage yet but my niece next to us has. Is there a delay with some cases?" Gavin asked.

"Let me check for you," confirmed the receptionist. "No, all the cases are being loaded on as normal. There's still some time before we sail, sir, I'm sure you will receive them soon," she continued

"Can I leave this with you in your safe?" asked Paul rather nervously, producing a small package from his pocket.

"Yes, of course, let me give you a receipt for it," the receptionist confirmed. "There we are, sir. Was there anything else?" she continued.

"No, that's fine," Paul said, thanking her.

Gavin had moved away from the desk and was admiring the atrium. The two of them walked up the central stairway and headed towards their cabins.

Louise knocked on her neighbour's cabin door. After what seemed a lifetime, the door opened and Helen stood before her.

"Oh, is there anything the matter?" asked Helen hesitantly.

"Please can I come in?" asked Louise.

"Yes, of course, sorry," Helen stepped aside and let Louise in.

"How would you like to join the five of us for drinks after our meal later tonight?" Louise asked, as she moved just inside the door.

Helen moved towards Neil further inside. She looked at Neil, almost for approval.

"Oh, that's very kind, isn't it, Neil?" asked Helen.

"Yes, it is, but are you sure you want us interrupting your evening?" Neil replied.

"Yes, it's fine. Anyway the youngsters probably won't stay that long," Louise retorted making light of it.

"Well, if you're sure, we'd be delighted," replied Helen, looking at Neil who smiled back.

"Great, shall we say around nine thirty? There's a sports bar a few decks down, I've seen on our ship's pocket map," Louise confirmed.

"Half nine it is then, and thank you again, Louise," Helen replied.

Louise opened the door and returned to her cabin.

6 – BON VOYAGE

CZN CRUISES
ATL17 – BISCAY HIGHLIGHTS
SUNDAY 24th JULY to SUNDAY 31st JULY

Sunday 24th July
Southampton, depart late afternoon; dress code, smart casual

Monday 25th July
Day at sea; dinner dress formal

Tuesday 26th July
Bilbao, arrive early morning; depart late afternoon; evening 80s night

Wednesday 27th July
Lisbon, arrive mid-morning; depart early evening; dress smart casual

Thursday 28th July
Day at sea; evening dress formal

Friday 29th July
La Rochelle, arrive early morning; depart late afternoon; dress smart casual

Saturday 30th July
Guernsey (tender), arrive mid-morning; depart mid-afternoon; dress smart casual

Sunday 31st July
Southampton, disembark early morning
EVENING DINNER
First sitting: 6.15 p.m.
Second sitting: 8.30 p.m.

CZN had prepared a party atmosphere for *the Atlantic* this season every time it sailed from Southampton. There were balloons, streamers, brass and pipe bands playing and even fireworks on selected cruises. When *the Atlantic* set sail, there were crowds of onlookers on the quayside, waving frantically at the passengers, who had decided to watch from the upper decks. The party atmosphere on board was interrupted by the tannoy system.

"Good afternoon, ladies and gentlemen, this is your Captain speaking and wishing you all a warm welcome to *the Atlantic*. I can confirm now all passengers and luggage are safely on board and as you can see, we are slowly sailing down the Solent. The weather forecast for the next few days is set fair for our sail across the Bay of Biscay tomorrow and we're not expecting the sea's swell to be problematic. Some of you may have heard stories of an ex-hurricane sweeping across the Atlantic Ocean sometime next week. We will, of course, be keeping a very close eye on this weather pattern and will keep you regularly updated. In the meantime, may I wish you a very pleasant evening on board and hope you enjoy your cruise with us in the coming week."

Gavin and Paul returned to their cabins at the same time as Sarah and they all joined Louise inside their cabin. Gavin and Louise's luggage had arrived now and Louise had started unpacking.

"Right, let's open that bottle of champagne," said Gavin.

"Don't forget you owe me a bottle as well after that bet. Now what was it you said at the time, Gavin? None of the cheap house plonk, I think," answered Louise with a huge smile. "Does Megan know we're all meeting up? Did you tell her when you saw her, Sarah?"

"Not exactly, but she knows where we are," Sarah replied.

"Sarah?" Louise quizzed. "I'll try the phone in her cabin."

Just then, there was a knock at the door. It was Megan. Gavin let her in.

"Where have you been? I was about to phone your cabin," asked Louise.

"I took a quick trip to the outside deck just as we were sailing away. There were streamers and balloons everywhere. I wish I'd taken a photo now," replied Megan.

Megan had brought a copy of the *News* in with her and was quickly given a glass of champagne by Gavin. They all raised their glasses to each other.

"Bon Voyage and happy cruising everyone!" said Gavin.

"I am looking forward to this cruise more than ever, now we're actually on board," said Louise excitedly. "What's that you brought in with you, Megan?"

"It was in your post tray outside your cabin. It looks like an events guide for the evening," Megan replied.

"And speaking of this evening, Louise has something to confer to the younger members of the party," Gavin retorted sarcastically.

"They don't have to stay all night, I'm sure," confirmed Louise, now looking straight at Gavin. "I've arranged for us to meet up with Helen and Neil for a drink after our meal tonight, because I think Helen could do with some moral support."

"Well, this could be explosive if our first meetings are anything to go by and if we're lucky, they'll have fallen out after five minutes and we'll be left alone anyway," remarked Paul.

"A few drinks won't hurt, I'm sure," responded Megan.

"He is married, you know," Sarah pointed out, aimed at Megan.

"Maybe not for much longer?" quizzed Paul smiling.

Megan looked at Sarah with 'daggers', but said nothing.

"Children, please!" shouted Louise. "Anyway, I've found something very interesting in this paper Megan brought in, Gavin. Read this." Louise passed the *News* across to Gavin who started reading at the bottom of the back page.

"Sounds good, but I'm supposed to be on holiday?" quizzed Gavin.

"I know, but wouldn't it be great to show other passengers some basics and pass on your knowledge and expertise about IT?" asked Louise. "What's the worst thing that can happen?"

"Famous last words, Louise, famous last words," Gavin said with a sigh because he knew what was coming.

Sarah, Paul and Megan all offered encouragement, simultaneously.

"That's settled then, we'll make enquiries before dinner this evening," confirmed Louise.

"I suppose it won't do any harm," replied Gavin in a resigned tone.

CZN had several dining options for its passengers. As well as the traditional same table, same time option in the main restaurant, there was another restaurant for flexible dining, buffet and theme-styled dining options, snack bars and also room service available each day. Sarah and family hadn't booked the traditional option, which left them to choose an option every day. Tonight, they had decided on a buffet meal near the top deck of *the Atlantic* before they headed down to meet Helen and Neil for drinks. First up though was the IT enquiry.

Sarah, Paul and Megan decided to try the sports bar and left Louise and Gavin to head for reception at the bottom of the atrium.

When they arrived at reception, they were greeted by a friendly receptionist.

"How can I help you, sir, madam?" she asked with a broad smile.

"I'd like to make an enquiry into your request for taking a couple of IT classes," Gavin said.

"Certainly, sir, and you're in luck because our Cruise Director is here now. Take a seat and I'll have him come over to see you very shortly," the receptionist confirmed.

"Oh alright, thank you," Gavin replied, somewhat surprised.

Louise and Gavin sat on some chairs at the side of reception. This was where future bookings were made, but it was empty at the moment. They looked up at the atrium, which was full of other passengers, three decks high and dominated this part of *the Atlantic.* As they were taking in the ambiance, Craig walked towards them.

"Hello, I'm Craig, the Cruise Director," as he put out his hand to greet them.

"Hi, I'm Gavin, and this is my wife, Louise," Gavin replied.

They all shook hands. Craig sat down beside them both.

"So, you're interested in taking some IT classes for us. Do you work in IT, Gavin?"

"Yes, I've been in IT for several years and I'm now a manager with a local authority."

"What we're looking for is someone who can teach our passengers the basics and introduce them to emails, the internet, searching websites, that sort of thing. It would be two thirty to forty minute classes but nothing too complicated or heavy. After all, our passengers are on holiday and we don't want them stressing!" Craig continued. "How does that sound?"

"It sounds fine, but don't you have other passengers who've volunteered?" quizzed Gavin, trying to stall somewhat.

"No, you're the first, Gavin, but time is against me and if you are experienced as you say you are, then I'm sure you'll be fine," Craig confirmed.

"What do you think, Louise?" Gavin asked, turning to his wife.

"It's up to you, Gavin, but I think you'll be great and you'll enjoy it!" beamed Louise.

"Well, if you're sure, Craig?" Gavin asked as if for final approval. "What happens now?"

"The first class is set for tomorrow afternoon at 2 p.m. with the follow-up class on Thursday when we're at sea again. I'll make the necessary arrangements and we'll make a tannoy announcement tonight and again in the morning, informing passengers the class will be going ahead. Please meet me here around 1 p.m. tomorrow and we'll go through the details of the class together. I'll have a Junior Officer accompany you in the class," Craig continued.

"All sounds very positive, Gavin," beamed Louise.

"Yes, you'll be fine, I'm sure," confirmed Craig.

"Right, well I'll see you tomorrow," Gavin replied.

The three of them stood up and shook hands.

"Thank you for volunteering, see you tomorrow," Craig confirmed, as he walked back to reception.

Gavin nodded and smiled at Louise as they made their way up the atrium stairway towards the sports bar. When they arrived, the three youngsters had found a table and were sipping their first drink of the evening.

"Over here!" Megan raised her hand.

Gavin and Louise wandered across. Almost immediately, a waiter was there to take their order.

"Two glasses of champagnes, please," Louise confirmed. "You're now looking at CZN's official IT teacher for the week."

"Did no one else respond?" asked Megan tongue-in-cheek.

"Megan!" Louise scolded.

"Joking, of course," Megan teased.

"Tell us all, Uncle," Sarah quizzed.

"It's nothing really, there's to be a half-hour class on the two days at sea going through the basics, including emails, internet and website searching, that kind of thing."

"Rather you than me, I don't think I could handle the attention," replied Paul.

"It's not the attention I worry about Paul, but more the subject matter and if anyone will benefit from it."

Just then, the drinks arrived.

"A toast to Gavin, our IT teacher!" Louise said while raising her glass.

Helen and Neil had decided not to have their evening dinner in the same restaurant each night either, and like Sarah's group had elected to choose for themselves where and when they ate. As this was their first cruise, they opted for the safe option and headed for the traditional themed pub for their first evening meal. It was filling up when they arrived. They grabbed a table and settled down looking at the menu.

"Louise seems a lovely person," Helen started. "It was kind of her to invite us for some drinks later."

"Yes, I'm looking forward to that," replied Neil grinning slightly.

"I hope we can enjoy ourselves on this cruise, a week's relaxation could be just the ticket for us both," Helen continued.

Neil nodded slightly but said nothing. The atmosphere was relaxed with anticipation of a relaxing week together. Before long, they had ordered their meal, had a few drinks in the bar and were looking forward to the evening ahead.

Sarah's group made their way up to the buffet restaurant for their meal. The sea was calm tonight and with a sea view, made for a relaxing meal together.

"How do we think tonight is going to go?" quizzed Sarah.

"Hopefully, longer than ten minutes," Gavin replied.

"Is there a feeling Helen and Gavin's marriage is in trouble?" asked Louise sarcastically.

"They can certainly argue," added Paul.

"All married couples argue, even Gavin and I!" Louise quickly added.

"That's what you two have to look forward to," Megan said, turning to Sarah and Paul.

"Anyway as I've said, I like Helen and I'm looking forward to meeting them later," Louise retorted. "You guys don't have to stay long if you don't want to."

Their excellent evening meal passed by quickly but was interrupted by an announcement on the loudspeaker.

"Good evening, ladies and gentlemen, I hope you are enjoying your first evening at sea with us. I am delighted to announce that our scheduled beginner's IT class will be taking part tomorrow as planned. A passenger has kindly volunteered and I'm sure you will give him all the support and encouragement required tomorrow afternoon in our IT classroom adjacent to the library. There is lots of entertainment this evening to choose from and I hope you all have a very pleasant evening."

"Listen to that, fame!" remarked Louise.

"Well, you know, what can I say, folks," Gavin said as he sat back in his seat.

"Never mind the fame, we're late for our drinks with Helen and Neil!" confirmed Paul looking at his watch. "It's past half nine now," he continued.

"Wow, I didn't realise it was so late. Quick, everyone, finish your drinks. We need to leave now!" Louise instructed.

Everyone took one final gulp of their drink and headed towards the sports bar. On arrival, Helen and Neil were already there and had managed to secure a table for seven in a corner with a couple of seats alongside.

"We're so sorry, Helen, we lost track of time," Louise confirmed, reaching the table first.

"Don't worry, you're here now."

Helen and Neil, having already had a few drinks, were feeling very relaxed. Louise sat down next to Helen in the corner with Gavin and then Sarah and Paul taking the final chairs. Megan sat beside Neil.

The drinks were soon flowing and as the night continued, the party of seven split into three. Helen and Louise struck up an immediate rapport and were laughing and giggling together, Gavin was talking to Sarah and Paul, and Neil and Megan were sitting on the end together talking with intermittent comments with Sarah and Paul. At brief moments, they would brush together in the corner seats, almost flirting but being careful not to make it obvious. Sometime later, Sarah and Paul declared they were ready for bed and made their excuses.

"We're going to retire now, it's been a long day," Sarah confirmed.

"Are you sure? It's still early. Paul, tell her not to be so boring," Louise said, slightly drunk herself and slurring out her words to Paul.

"More than my life's worth to argue, Louise," Paul said, keeping the peace.

"We'll see you tomorrow then," Gavin confirmed to them both.

"Will do," replied Sarah.

Don't do anything I wouldn't," Megan said sarcastically.

Neil laughed and looked at Megan.

"Megan?" Louise asked.

"See you tomorrow," confirmed Sarah again as she walked with Paul hand in hand away from the sports bar and towards their cabin.

Neil, now realising the environment had changed, suggested a change of venue.

"Anyone fancy our chances at the casino?"

"Now you're talking," Helen replied enthusiastically.

"You play cards or roulette, Helen?" Louise asked quite surprised.

"When I can, I love blackjack."

"Casino it is then," said Neil and rose from the table with Megan.

The casino was right across from the bar and was quite busy with passengers trying their luck. Helen and Louise found two seats at the blackjack table and sat down to play. Gavin wasn't interested so he decided to just watch.

"Drinks anyone?" asked Megan rather innocently.

"One for the road, eh Helen," suggested Louise, now quite drunk.

"I'll give you a hand," confirmed Gavin.

"Let me get this round, on Helen and I," said Neil, now moving back towards the sports bar.

Neil, Gavin and Megan ordered the drinks from the bar. Gavin took Helen and Louise's drinks across to them, leaving Megan and Neil at the bar. Neil continued the charm offensive.

"I think I've had one too many tonight," confirmed Megan nudging Neil away.

"Come on, Megan, and anyway as your aunt said, one for the road."

"No, I'm going to suffer tomorrow as it is," Megan confirmed. "I'm going to let Gavin and Louise know I'm leaving."

Neil waited for their drinks and followed Megan back to the casino. Megan said goodnight to everyone and left for her cabin. The four older adults stayed for a while longer before retiring for the night themselves.

7 – GRAND TOUR

Megan was having trouble with her head! As well as having one drink too many last night, it had been her first night at sea and she was suffering badly! A glance at her watch revealed she was late for the tour of *the Atlantic* they were all going to attend this morning at 11 a.m. Her watch revealed it was 11.30 a.m! A quick shower and a strong, black coffee would hopefully change all that.

Sandra was a no-nonsense Dundonian in her mid-thirties who had been with CZN for nearly ten years now and had progressed to Head Tour Rep, after transferring from a smaller ship in the fleet. It was her job to manage the other reps and she reported directly to the Cruise Director, Craig.

"Are you ready for our tour this morning, Sharon?" she asked her fellow Tour Guide on board.

"Yes, thanks, Sandra. Ready to go," Sharon replied.

"Good, we'll split into two groups depending on how many numbers we get this morning. I will start at the atrium and work my way up finishing at Nevis's bar. You do the reverse, starting from Nevis's and finishing at the atrium," instructed Sandra as they walked together to the atrium. There was a large group of passengers awaiting their arrival. Sarah, Paul, Louise and Gavin had assembled themselves between reception and the atrium stairs.

"Do you think Megan is OK?" Louise quizzed the others.

"She's probably lying low, finding her sea legs," replied Gavin. "We'll check on her after the tour if she doesn't surface beforehand."

Sandra made her way towards reception while Sharon moved to the stairs.

"Let the passengers know what's going on, Sharon. I'll be over in a minute," Sandra instructed.

"Good morning, ladies and gentlemen, and welcome to *the Atlantic*," Sharon started in a polite and confident manner. "I will be your tour guide this morning along with my colleague, Sandra. We are going to split you all into two groups and this tour of our wonderful ship will last approximately an hour, finishing at midday."

Just as Sandra was moving across towards Sharon to start the tour, an announcement rang out from the tannoy.

"Good morning, ladies and gentlemen. Can I remind all passengers that our planned IT class for beginners scheduled for 2 p.m. this afternoon will go ahead as planned and will be taken by a fellow passenger who has kindly volunteered. I'm sure you'll want to give him your support in our IT classroom next to the library this afternoon."

"Was last night's announcement not enough for the passengers?" asked Paul.

"Sometimes they need a nudge in the right direction," Gavin confirmed with a wry smile.

"Don't get too confident, it doesn't suit you, Uncle," Sarah laughed.

Sandra and Sharon were preparing to start the tour. The passengers were now split into two groups. Sarah and her family would be starting at the atrium with Sandra and work up the ship's decks towards Nevis's bar where the tour finished.

Megan's shower had helped somewhat, but she still needed that coffee and although there were facilities in her cabin, she decided to leave it and find a quiet corner in a coffee bar one deck below her cabin. Megan walked slowly along the corridor and towards the atrium stairs, but she wasn't looking where she was going and when she reached the top of the stairs, she bumped into someone else coming up.

"Oh, sorry I wasn't looking where I was going," she said sheepishly, looking up to reveal a young man who had been walking up the stairs towards her.

"That's fine, are you OK?" the young man asked softly.

"Yes, fine, thanks," replied Megan who was slightly embarrassed now and started her descent down the staircase.

"Are you OK? You're having a laugh, she virtually ran you over!" screeched George at his older brother.

"No harm done," replied Henry.

"Oh my god, first impressions and all that. You like her, don't you?" George asked.

Henry just stared back at George, saying nothing.

"She is so out of your league," George said, mocking his brother.

"Is that a challenge?" Henry countered, feeling slightly bolder. "Only if she looks back when she reaches the bottom of the stairs, though I deserve a sporting chance if she's out of my league?" he continued with a hint of sarcasm.

Henry was gambling with George that he would accept his counter challenge. Megan walked down the stairs and paused slightly as they banked to the left halfway down. She continued towards the bottom. The chance encounter with Henry had intrigued Megan and just as she left the stairs, she glanced behind her and up towards the brothers who were now looking straight back at her.

Henry just smiled back at Megan, while the adrenalin rushed inside him. He paused for a second...

"Game on then, George?" he asked, almost dismissing the whole event, but knowing his younger brother wouldn't be able to resist.

"You bet, big brother!" George shouted as he offered a high-five.

"What are you two boys up to now?" asked their mother, Mary.

"Oh, nothing, just playing around," replied Henry.

The two brothers looked at each other and smiled. The family walked back towards their suite. They had booked only one of two suites on *the Atlantic*. Henry and his younger brother George were on a family cruise celebrating two birthdays. Henry would be twenty-one on Saturday while their father, John, was sixty the following week. Their suite was laid out across two decks and had a piano on the lower floor, with a large balcony and living area. Upstairs were two bedrooms and a separate bath and shower room. The family had cruised before and lived in Poole, Dorset where they had a yacht in the marina.

Sandra started her tour at the bottom of the atrium stairs and walked up towards the upper decks. There were around 20 in each group. Sharon's group went first because they had to start from Nevis's bar. As they filtered up the stairs, a passenger came rushing through. It was Rebecca.

"Is this the tour of the ship?" she asked breathlessly.

"Yes, madam, it is. Just follow me up these stairs," replied Sharon.

"How long is the tour for?" asked Rebecca again.

"About an hour, but we're finishing at noon sharp so if you'd like to come along, madam," Sandra now intervened.

Sandra continued the tour up the decks. Her group was growing in size with each deck they entered. They passed along the shops, casino, sports bar, theatre and cinema, library, IT classroom where Gavin was going to be hosting his first class later, and then they continued to the outside swimming pools, sports decks, health spa area and the many other attractions on offer.

"I didn't realise how much there is to do on the ship," Louise remarked.

"Hannah and I were never bored on our cruise last year and that ship was smaller than this one," confirmed Sarah.

When they reached the outside decks, the weather was breezy but clear and by this time, a sizeable crowd was following Sandra as she reached Nevis's bar.

"This is the end of our tour, ladies and gentlemen. I hope you will be able to find your way around *the Atlantic* a bit easier now. There are maps of the ship on each deck beside the lifts and stairways, but please ask a member of the crew if you are unsure about anything," confirmed Sandra as she addressed the large group of passengers.

The passengers quickly dispersed. Sandra headed back to check on Sharon, leaving Sarah and her family group at Nevis's bar.

"Seems a shame to leave the bar while we're here," quizzed Gavin.

"Should we not try and find Megan?" asked Louise.

"Yes, but she could be anywhere and she knows where the class is. We'll look for her after my class if we don't see her beforehand," Gavin replied.

"OK, but no later," Louise confirmed.

The atmosphere was interrupted by the tannoy and a bell ringing.

"Good afternoon, ladies and gentlemen. It is 12 o'clock noon and this is your Captain speaking. I very much hope you're enjoying your first morning with us on board *the Atlantic*. As you can see, the weather is being kind to us today as we head down the Bay of Biscay towards our first port of call in Bilbao tomorrow morning. Yesterday I mentioned the possibility of a hurricane later in the week. Our latest reports suggest that it will lose strength over the coming days and its exact course may change slightly away from our position. We are still monitoring the situation closely and I will, of course, keep you informed. May I remind all passengers that a fellow passenger is taking our beginner's course in IT this afternoon so I'm sure you will give him your encouragement and support in our IT classroom at 2 p.m. And please remember tonight's dress is formal attire. It just remains for me to wish you all a very enjoyable afternoon in whatever you decide to do for the remainder of the day."

"What did you bribe them with to have the Captain mention your class again?" asked Sarah, slightly jealous.

Gavin's mind had temporarily wandered into stardom.

"That's the problem with fame. Some people get one whiff of it and become totally self-obsessed," he said.

"Pardon? Earth calling Gavin, where are you?" Louise asked now mocking.

"Oh sorry, was a bit carried away there!"

"Right, who's up for a drink with an ocean view?" asked Sarah rather excitedly.

"Would be rude not to," Paul answered back.

The four of them sat by the bar and ordered a snack lunch and a round of drinks.

Megan reached the coffee bar shortly after her encounter with Henry at the top of the stairs and found a quiet corner. She ordered a strong black coffee, which came in no time. The coffee took effect immediately and she was feeling better already, although her head was a bit delicate. Not one for holiday romances, she smiled to herself as she ordered another coffee. She hadn't been on *the Atlantic* one day, yet already she had come into close proximity with two gentlemen, and on first impressions they couldn't be further apart, certainly in terms of persona and appearance. The young man on the stairs was the younger of the two, well-built and had sounded very well spoken and courteous, enough to ask how she was, even though it was her fault. Yet there was a forbidden attraction towards Neil, even though she knew it was wrong at every level. It wouldn't do any harm, she thought, to keep her options open though. As her second coffee arrived, she started contemplating just how intriguing this cruise could become in the coming days.

8 – IT @ 2

With their lunch finished at Nevis's, Gavin and Louise made their way back down towards the atrium to meet Craig at 1 p.m. as arranged. Sarah and Paul stayed at Nevis's for another drink but promised to be at the class in plenty of time. Craig was waiting for them when they arrived.

"Hi Gavin, Louise, nice to meet you again. Are you feeling OK Gavin? No last minute nerves?" Craig asked in a friendly tone.

"Too late for that now, even if I did," replied Gavin.

"You'll be fine," Louise said, giving encouragement.

"Absolutely. I've spoken to a lot of passengers and I reckon they'll be around two dozen attending this afternoon, which I reckon is a good-sized class for you to start with," Craig confirmed. "I've arranged for Sahid, one of our Junior Officers, to meet us there before the class starts, and he will be with you as support throughout the class. All the material you need is there for you, Gavin, so if you're ready, we'll make our way up now," Craig continued.

"Right, sooner we start," Gavin confirmed as he took a gulp.

"Good man!" shouted Craig.

The three of them made the short trip up the stairs to the IT classroom beside the library. Sahid was ready to meet them in the room.

"Sahid, this is Gavin who's taking our class this afternoon, and his wife, Louise. Gavin, this is Sahid, our Junior Officer," said Craig, starting the introductions.

"Pleasure to meet you, sir," said Sahid, shaking hands with Gavin and Louise.

"It's Gavin from now on."

Sahid nodded and smiled.

"There are about fifteen PCs, so depending on numbers, some people might have to share. You will be here at the front using this PC. Have a quick look in the folders, which will tell you what you'll be touching on during your class. As I mentioned, don't worry if you go beyond the scheduled thirty minutes, unless you feel you've finished. Remember to keep it light-hearted and relaxing throughout. I can't stay, I'm afraid, but with Sahid you are in very capable hands. I will come back afterwards to see how you've done. Don't worry, Gavin, you'll be fine."

With that, Craig left the room, leaving Gavin, Louise and Sahid.

"Right, let's get started," said Gavin, rather confidently despite butterflies starting inside his stomach.

"I'm going to stay with you up front," Louise confirmed.

"Yes, thanks, that will be fine. What about yourself, Sahid?" Gavin asked.

"Hopefully nobody is going to notice I'm here!" he confirmed. "I'll float round the room watching the proceedings, but helping if and when required."

The first passengers were beginning to arrive and three of them were very familiar.

"You've risen from the land of the dead, then?" asked Gavin, now looking at Megan.

"Where have you been?" Louise asked.

"Sorry, I overslept then I needed a strong coffee, but look who I bumped into en route," she turned, revealing Helen and Neil.

"Aw, thank you for coming, you two. I'm sure you have better things to do this afternoon," Louise said.

"Wouldn't miss it for the world! Anyway, happy to lend any support we can," confirmed Helen, as they moved towards the back of the class.

Megan chose a PC near the front just as Sarah and Paul arrived, who decided for a spot towards the rear. The class was filling up and it was nearly time to start. Just before Gavin started, an elderly couple entered the room.

"Sorry we're late," the lady said, sounding out of breath.

"That's quite alright," Gavin confirmed. "We'll give it a couple of minutes."

Although almost full, there were two spare seats beside Megan towards the front.

"Come across here, dear, beside this young lady," the elderly lady said to her husband. They settled down beside Megan.

"It's my uncle taking this class, you know," Megan confirmed excitedly.

"Oh excellent! Did you hear that, John? It's this young lady's uncle who's teaching us today. Oh, that is a relief, I wasn't sure how this was going to go. It's more for my husband than me. I'm Mary, by the way, and it's very nice to meet you."

"It's Megan, and the pleasure is mine."

"Oh, this is excellent because if we're not sure about anything, we can ask Megan here, John, and I'm sure she'll keep us right. Won't you, dear?" Mary asked.

"Yes, of course, but Gavin's very good, you know, so you'll be fine," Megan replied.

"Oh, that's wonderful, my husband has his own business, you see and really needs to be brought into the twenty-first century, don't you, John?"

John nodded and smiled back at Megan. Just then, Sahid started the class.

"Good afternoon, ladies and gentlemen, and welcome to our IT class for beginners. My name is Sahid and, as you know, Gavin has kindly volunteered after a staff illness, so I'm sure the next thirty minutes or so will be very informative and enjoyable. Gavin."

"Thank you, Sahid," started Gavin, very nervously. "My remit this afternoon, ladies and gentlemen, is to show you the basics of email and websites and the internet in general, and our class is to last about half an hour, but I've been told we can take longer if required."

The class soon developed a pattern. Gavin was at the front with Louise helping any passengers needing assistance. Megan had struck up a rapport with John and Mary at the front and was guiding them when required. Sarah, Paul, Helen and Neil sat at the back. Before long, Gavin was wrapping up the class and after a rapture of applause from the passengers, small groups were forming as some passengers left and others started conversations. Unknown to Gavin, Craig had managed to return earlier than planned and saw the final minutes of the class for himself through the door window.

"Are you only with your aunt and uncle?" Mary asked Megan.

"No, there's five of us in total, My cousin is with her boyfriend."

"Well, you've been very patient with us this afternoon, Megan, and your uncle would make an excellent teacher. Was this his first time taking a class?"

"I think so, certainly one like this," replied Megan.

Craig had entered the room and initially spoke to Sahid before heading towards Gavin.

"How did you enjoy that, Gavin?" he asked.

"After a few early nerves, I think it went quite well," Gavin replied.

"Oh, I can tell it went well from the atmosphere within the room. You'll take the follow-up class on Thursday?" Craig asked, wasting no time.

"I don't see why not," confirmed Gavin.

"Of course he will, knock them out," beamed Louise.

"Thank you very much for such an informative class, Gavin. I know John has learned much today and your niece has been excellent with us oldies," said Mary.

"I'm glad you enjoyed it. Can I expect you on Thursday?" Gavin asked, now growing in confidence.

"You bet!" Mary confirmed as she walked towards the door. John shook Gavin's hand and followed his wife out.

"Well, when's the fan club starting?" teased Sarah.

There was a pause before laughter within the group.

"Gavin, I have to go, but you and your family will join me for drinks later tonight on CZN, of course?" asked Craig.

"Well, if you're sure?" Gavin replied, rather sheepishly.

"We'll be there, tell us where and when, thanks!" Louise intervened.

"Excellent, there's a champagne bar not far from here. Have you been in it yet?"

"I don't think so, but I think I know the one you mean," Gavin replied.

"Right, well let's say around 11 o'clock. I'll see you all then."

Craig left with Sahid, leaving Sarah's party with Helen and Neil.

"You'll join us later, Helen?" asked Louise.

"Oh, I don't know, it's a family thing, I think," she confirmed.

"Afterwards then?" Louise persisted.

"Yes, maybe, I'm not sure what we're doing yet."

With that, they all left the IT classroom together.

9 – BLACK AND WHITE

John and Mary were experienced cruisers with many years and subsequent loyalty bonuses with CZN behind them. John had owned his own stockbroking business in Poole for many years but was looking towards retirement, or at least, taking a back seat as he approached his sixtieth birthday. His eldest son, Henry, had recently started working in the business and was effectively running it on his father's behalf. The family were well known to CZN and traditionalists when it came to cruising, always dining in the main restaurant at the second sitting. Formal nights were a chance for the family to 'hit the town', and with a champagne reception organised by CZN for its loyal passengers afterwards, it was an evening to look forward to.

"Come on, boys. We don't want to be late," instructed Mary as she hurried them all along.

Although John was the head of the house and family, it was Mary who ran the household and was the link between her husband and the two boys, who were growing up fast. As the eldest son, Henry was always going to work in the family business and attended an all-boys school before studying business at university. His younger brother, George, was something of a rebel and although had attended the same school as Henry, he was seeking his fortune elsewhere and certainly well beyond the family business.

"First chance to see that girl again tonight then?" he mocked at Henry.

"No pressure, plenty of time. This is a marathon, not a sprint," Henry replied.

"You don't even know her name or anything about her," George continued.

"Makes the challenge more intriguing," Henry confirmed.

63

The family made their way towards the main restaurant. The attire on show tonight was a sea of black and white as passengers rose to the occasion on this first formal night of the cruise. Men were mainly in white shirt, black bow tie and suit, although the occasional white jacket added a certain colour to the evening. Ladies were ever slightly more colourful but they had more discretion on offer.

Craig had a busy evening. Together with the Captain, he was hosting the champagne reception for CZN's more loyal customers, which was due to start just after 10 p.m., and then he had arranged to meet Gavin, Louise and family for a drink, an hour later. At least it was in the same place, he thought. The reception was going well and the champagne was flowing.

"I thoroughly enjoyed the IT class today. Gavin was very informative and his niece was very helpful," Mary said to Craig.

"Yes, we struck gold with Gavin when he volunteered last night."

"How is the new ship coming along now that she's been sailing for nearly three months?" Mary asked, making small talk.

"We're very happy with the reaction of our passengers and media so far," Craig replied.

"I can't see your young lady here," remarked George towards Henry.

"Oh, it's young lady now! It was a girl earlier."

"Whatever!" George retorted.

The family left the reception shortly before 11 o'clock and made their way back to their mini suite. George was first to spot a familiar face as they reached the top of the stairs.

"Isn't that your young lady going to where we've just left?" he asked Henry.

Henry turned round but only caught a glimpse as she walked away from them and one deck below.

"Not sure, but there's plenty of opportunity tomorrow," he smiled as they both walked away.

The last of the reception passengers had left the bar and it was opened up to any remaining passengers for a late drink. The Captain had also departed, leaving Craig on his own, albeit temporarily. Gavin, Louise and family entered the bar and quickly spotted Craig.

"Hello, again. Glad you could make it," he said to welcome them all. "What would you like to drink?"

"Champagne all round, I think," confirmed Louise.

"If that's OK?" Gavin countered.

"Yes, of course," Craig continued, and ordered at the bar. "One of our passengers was just praising your class this afternoon. She was very impressed, Gavin. You've certainly made an impression there."

"Oh, beginner's luck, perhaps." Gavin was slightly embarrassed.

"Will you excuse me, thanks?" Craig asked the party. It had been a long day and there was one final meeting before the night was done.

"Yes, of course, we're fine here, and thanks for the drink," Louise confirmed.

"Good, I'll see you before Thursday's class, I hope," said Craig as he moved to the end of the bar where another young woman was sitting. It was clear he had met her before. Craig sat down beside her. Just then, two other familiar faces entered the bar. It was Helen and Neil.

"So glad you could make it," Louise said as they sat down beside them at the bar. "You two scrub up well," she teased slightly.

"You have to make the effort on formal nights, although I think a few passengers haven't," Neil stated.

"It's a pity, because I do like dressing up on these occasions," Helen continued. "Anyway, one could say the same about you two and the youngsters behind you."

Sarah and Paul watched Craig with the other woman at the bar and Sarah was intrigued.

"You know that feeling when you think you've seen someone before but you can't place them?" Sarah continued.

"Yes, go on," Paul replied enthusiastically.

"She has a familiar face and it's going to annoy me if I can't place her."

"Wasn't she the passenger who turned up late for the tour earlier today?" Paul asked.

"Yes, you're right, but that's not where I'm thinking," Sarah confirmed, still rather puzzled.

After their initial drink at the bar, Helen and Neil were ready to leave for the night.

"Are you going already?" asked Louise.

"Yes, it's been a long day and tomorrow is another long one," replied Helen, looking rather tired.

Megan exchanged a quick glance with Neil as he left with Helen. There would be no 'flirting' tonight. She had also seen the young lady with Craig and recognised her as Rebecca who she had met that first time at her cabin. I think I'll just hold back any information for now, thought Megan. I'm sure this isn't going to be the last encounter with her, and if it's puzzling Sarah somewhat, then that's something of a bonus. Megan smiled to herself as Craig and Rebecca parted.

10 – EXCURSION EXODUS

It was early morning when *the Atlantic* slipped into Bilbao. The passengers had a full day here, and with the weather set to be hot and sunny, more than half of the passengers on board would either be booked on an excursion or taking a trip off the ship somewhere themselves.

Sarah and family had elected for a part coach, part walking tour of Bilbao's highlights, which would last a full morning and part of the afternoon. This would leave enough time to either explore some more of Bilbao or relax back on the ship and enjoy the sunshine. Henry, George and his parents were booked on a cultural tour, visiting the modern Guggenheim Museum before a guided tour around the Old Quarter. Helen and Neil were on a full day's coach tour around the vineyards, and with free samples included, they were looking forward to it.

Sandra was one of the reps going round the vineyards. Two buses were ready for the passengers and there was an air of excitement when the coaches set off. It was a couple of hours before they reached the first vineyard. Sandra stood up on her coach as it entered the coach park.

"OK, ladies and gentlemen, we have just under an hour here. There will be an opportunity for wine tasting at the end. Please ensure you are all back on the coach in an hour. Thank you."

"We have certainly landed lucky today, Neil. What could be better than local wine in the sun?"

"A massive hangover, if we're not careful, and remember the party on board later. We don't want to miss that," Neil replied to his wife as they strolled towards the winery.

As the day progressed, the atmosphere on the coach seemed to become a bit louder as each vineyard and wine tasting passed.

67

They stopped for lunch, but this didn't seem to halt the flow. The combination of wine and sun was taking its toll. By mid-afternoon, some passengers were dancing on the coach, which Sandra didn't take too kindly to.

"May I please remind passengers, they must remain seated on the coach at all times," she barked out loud.

"Aw, come on, Sandra! We're just having a bit of fun," Helen replied.

There was much cheering from the coach. The majority of passengers were of a more mature age with Helen and Neil being one of the youngest couples. The ones that were still awake were more than making up for others who were having a siesta!

Helen hadn't heeded her husband's advice and was now more than tipsy and slurring her words.

"I do love you, you know that, don't you?" she said to Neil.

"Yes, I know you do," Neil replied, realising Helen was now properly drunk.

"Do you not love me?" was the inevitable response to Neil's silence.

"Yes, of course, but you're rather drunk, so this isn't the time."

There was one final vineyard before the coaches made their way back to *the Atlantic*. Some of the passengers were asleep when the bus pulled up at the last venue and were left on the coach. On the final road back, the singing was louder than ever, but by now the passengers were heeding Sandra's earlier instructions. Helen had fallen asleep and was slouched back against Neil who was trapped in his seat. On arrival back at the ship, it was late afternoon and the happy passengers made their way slowly back to their cabins. Helen was almost carried by Neil, who flopped down on the bed to sleep it off. Neil left her and made his way to the sun decks for some more sun.

Henry and George had come to a family compromise with their parents. In return for a morning excursion around Bilbao, it had been agreed the rest of the day was theirs, which included the party at sea later that evening. It had been their mother, Mary, who had brokered the deal. Both brothers had a strict upbringing with their father, John, very much 'old-school'. Their mother, on the other hand, was slightly younger than her husband and much more lenient and sympathetic towards the boys' recreational pursuits. The morning had been a cultural education for them both, starting at the Guggenheim.

"Tonight could be your lucky night, big brother," George mocked as they had walked around the museum.

"We'll see," Henry replied, secretly feeling excited but not wanting to show George. "You'll have to leave early, of course; the party will finish well past your bedtime."

"If that's true, you'll have to come back with me. You can't be trusted on your own," George continued the offensive. Henry just laughed back.

"What's all the hilarity, boys? You're supposed to be listening to your audio guides," their mother scolded.

The morning passed quickly and soon the excursion was over and the family were back on the ship. Before they went their separate ways for the afternoon, the family ate a late lunch in a snack bar on one of the higher decks inside.

Sarah, Paul, Louise and Gavin had also decided to stay within Bilbao on their tour, which ended at the Guggenheim Museum and gave them the choice to stay in the city or stay with the coach to go back to the ship. As it was a beautiful day, the chance of an extended walk was too good to miss.

"I'm still puzzled about that woman I saw last night," Sarah confirmed.

"Don't think about it and you'll remember," Gavin replied.

"I still think it was from the tour of the ship we took yesterday," Paul said, reiterating his comment from last night.

The four of them made their way towards a corner where something caught Gavin's eye.

"Now that's not something you see every day," he said, looking across the street.

A nun was talking into a mobile phone having a conversation while standing outside the convent. A minute or too later, a taxi pulled alongside and the nun got in while still talking on the phone.

"I wonder who she's talking to?" asked Louise, rather perplexed.

Gavin responded as quick as a flash.

"Why, God, of course!"

The nun was looking at them when she passed in the taxi, while the family party laughed at Gavin's instant response!

There was a shuttle coach service operating all day and the four decided the walk back to the ship was too far in the afternoon heat, so they took advantage of the air-conditioned shuttle and cooled off on their way back. With the thought of the night before in her head, Sarah decided to walk round the sun decks on the chance this intriguing woman might be there and she could find out where she knew her from.

11 - SUN LOUNGERS AND INTRIGUING INTERRUPTIONS

Megan had quickly realised that on a hot and sunny day, the best option was to cool off around the pool and have a quiet and relaxing day to herself. With so many passengers away on excursions, her chances of a poolside seat were greatly improved. Having seen the rest of her family off the ship, she made straight for the pool on the upper sun deck, and in no time she had found the perfect sun lounger halfway between the pool and Nevis's bar.

The morning couldn't have been more relaxing. The occasional dip in the pool, a constant stream of drinks supplied by attendant waiting staff, and a few hours of serious sunbathing was exactly the tonic she needed after finding her sea legs the night before last. This peace and quiet was inevitably not going to last, and soon she had a sun lounger companion.

"Am I alright to sit here for a while?" asked a familiar voice.

At first, Megan didn't see who it was because of the sun, but the shadowy figure soon revealed herself to be Rebecca.

"Yes, of course, there's no one using it," Megan replied.

Rebecca settled down, having placed some of her things at the side. There was a short pause before she started the conversation.

"Alone again? If I wasn't such a cynic, I'd suspect your family were imaginary."

Megan laughed. "Oh no, they exist alright. In fact, my cousin, Sarah, thinks she knows you from a previous life."

There was another short silence.

"Intriguing. Whereabouts is she from?" Rebecca asked, slightly hesitantly.

"Oxford," replied Megan. "We saw you last night with Craig, the Cruise Director."

"First name terms with Craig already?" Rebecca asked, deflecting the subject matter.

"My uncle, Gavin, took that IT class yesterday and we were invited for drinks as a thank you. How do you know Craig?"

"Oh, I'm a magazine reporter writing an article about *the Atlantic* and I've known Craig for a few years now."

"Some girls have all the luck, lounging around on cruises living the high life!" Megan replied slightly jealous.

"Some you win, some you lose."

It was approaching lunchtime and Megan needed food to soak up those drinks she had enjoyed earlier. The two of them strolled across to Nevis's bar and ordered a sandwich. The atmosphere between them was relaxed and friendly. The more Megan learned about Rebecca, the more she liked her, and keeping her cousin's frustration in mind was certainly helping.

Rebecca was enjoying the company. Being a reporter could often be lonely, and the company of another female of a similar era (although, she was seven years older than Megan) was an added bonus. Lunch finished, the two of them wandered back across to their sun loungers.

Henry and George had the rest of the day to themselves. What better place to start than on the outside decks in the early afternoon sunshine? They headed towards Nevis's bar for a refreshing drink. George sat down first with the best view of the open decks. Henry was facing the bar and caught the waiter's eye.

"I'll have a half lager and a coke for my brother."

"Sorry, a coke?" screeched George.

"Ok, a half lager for him as well," confirmed Henry backtracking.

"Very good, sir," confirmed the waiter as he smiled to himself walking back to Nevis's.

It wasn't long before George had clocked a familiar face.

"You're aware of the art of subtly, aren't you, Henry?"

"In what context?"

"You know the girl you met the other day, the one you have no chance with?"

Henry started to look round.

"Subtly remember, subtly, big brother!" Henry turned back facing George.

"Where are your sunglasses?" asked George.

"I've left them in our suite. Anyway, I'm fine," Henry replied slightly mumbling.

"You're so naïve, I'm not meaning for the sun!"

The waiter brought their drinks.

"Sunglasses have two functions, to protect your eyes from the sun and to view people without anyone knowing you are watching them."

Henry looked back slightly puzzled.

"Never mind that for now. She's there with another female, slightly older and not as pretty. When I say, have a look to your right and glance round, but remember Henry, be subtle."

George gave the word and Henry scanned the horizon and caught a glimpse of Megan and Rebecca who were sunbathing.

"How do you know it's her?" he asked.

"Trust me, it is, but the question is what are you going to do about it?" George pressed.

"Right this minute, nothing, but I can't believe she won't be at the party tonight."

"If it was me, I'd be there now introducing myself," confirmed George.

"Thankfully, I'm not you, George, and I play the long game," Henry replied.

The two brothers continued their drinks but their presence hadn't gone unnoticed.

"I think at least one of us has an admirer," confirmed Rebecca as she turned to Megan.

Megan had a quick look round towards the bar and recognised the brothers from yesterday.

"Oh god, I literally walked straight into one of them the other day!"

Rebecca just laughed which set Megan off.

"All I can say is if it was the older guy on the left, then I could think of worse figures to walk into," Rebecca said.

Henry was wearing a t-shirt and shorts and what he lacked in confidence, he more than made up for in physique. His years playing rugby at school and natural height were serving him well. On the other hand, his younger brother George may be the bold, confident one, but lacked Henry's physical attractions.

"My thoughts exactly, but at the time I wasn't looking where I was going because I was suffering from the night before," confirmed Megan.

A table had become free between the brother's and another couple at Nevis's, which gave Rebecca an idea.

"I'm going to sit at that free table and order a drink. Let's see if anything happens?"

Just at that moment, another familiar face approached them. It was Sarah.

"Ah, I'm glad I've found you, Megan."

There was a pause.

"Rebecca, this is my cousin, Sarah. Sarah, this is Rebecca."

"Do you know each other?" Sarah pressed.

"We met each other when I found my cabin the other day."

"Do I know you from somewhere?" Sarah pressed again.

"I don't think so, as far as I know," Rebecca replied.

"Funny because I'm sure I've seen you before. Never mind, it will come to me eventually," Sarah confirmed. "What do you do?"

"I'm a cruise magazine reporter writing an article about *the Atlantic*," Rebecca confirmed.

"Ah, I wondered when we saw you with Craig last night," Sarah continued. She turned to Megan. "Are you coming to the party later tonight?"

"I don't see why not, are you?"

"Yes, I think we're all going," Sarah responded. "Well, I'm sure I'll see you later, Megan. Nice to meet you, Rebecca."

"Likewise," Rebecca said.

With that, Sarah left.

"I'm sensing some tension between you two?" Rebecca asked softly.

"Not really, but I do get on much better with her younger sister. Do you recognise her?"

"I think I do, but it's my younger sister she knows and I wasn't going to let on just yet," Rebecca confirmed.

"Excellent, keeping my cousin guessing is fine by me!"

Henry, and more especially George, were sitting at Nevis's bar watching these activities while continuing with their drinks.

"Where were we, before we were so rudely interrupted?" quizzed Megan.

"I was going to take that table in between your admirers and another couple, and as it's still free, that's where I'm going now," Rebecca confirmed.

"OK, see you in a bit."

Rebecca strolled across to Nevis's and ordered a drink. Megan was left alone on her sun lounger.

"Strategies for tonight, Henry?" asked George.

"Not sure yet, still deciding."

"You might want to think about it soon, big brother, because I think you may have competition." George watched through his sunglasses as an older man approached and sat down on the sun lounger next to Megan.

Neil had spotted Megan and sauntered casually across to where she was lying back on the lounger. As there was a free one beside her, he sat down.

"You didn't fancy an excursion today?" he asked.

"Oh, hello, Neil. No, I've been enjoying some sunshine and relaxation. Where's Helen?"

"We've been on a vineyard trip and I think together with the sun, it's taken its toll. She's sleeping it off now. Anyway, it gives us some time together."

"For what exactly?"

"You weren't backing off the other night."

"I think I did, and anyway I had too much to drink and you're a happily married man."

"Who said anything about happily, and does that matter?"

"You don't love Helen anymore?"

"She's not the perfect ten, if that's what you mean."

"Tell me anyone who is? Look around you. There are numerous couples here who have probably been married for twenty, thirty years, and if you were to ask them, I bet they wouldn't score each other a ten either, but they're still together. I'm not sure I know what constitutes a ten anyway?"

"Come on then, score me out of ten?"

"Probably about seven."

"I'm only worth seven!"

"Don't flatter yourself, you're married and anyway, I've met someone else."

Neil paused for a second or two before responding. Megan was clearly playing hard to get.

"Met someone else already on the ship? You don't hang about, do you?"

"What can I say? Maybe I'm a ten."

"Looking forward to meeting him tonight then?"

"Yes, I'll see you later."

Neil stood up and walked away. Megan's afternoon had suddenly become rather frustrating and she was thinking about leaving the sun deck. Rebecca returned to find out the gossip and to report back about the brother's conversations.

"Well, if these two are brothers, then they're definitely chalk and cheese," Rebecca confirmed.

"Why, what have you found out?" asked Megan excitedly.

"The eldest is Henry and he's quite shy. Let's just say George, who although younger, is more streetwise and probably takes the lead between the two. Anyway, who was that just now?"

"No one really. He and his wife have a cabin which is in between Sarah, who you've just met, and my aunt and uncle. Was that all you were able to learn?"

"Yes, because the couple at the other table were interfering with their conversation," Rebecca confirmed, rather frustrated as well.

It had been a long, if not relaxing day, and Megan was gathering her things to leave for a second time with Rebecca when a third person approached them, which was totally unexpected. Rebecca decided to leave and said her goodbyes to Megan. They agreed to meet each other later that evening at the party.

"Come on, time to go. I can't get anywhere near her, even if I wanted to," said Henry to George. "I still have plenty of time though," he continued.

The two brothers left Nevis's to wander around other parts of the ship, contemplating tonight's open deck party.

Helen couldn't sleep when her husband had left her and after a quick coffee in her cabin, she decided to go for a wander herself. She had been contemplating her cruise with Neil and where her life was going. This cruise was a make-or-break holiday and there was someone she wanted to talk to. On locating her, she walked across to where she was sitting gathering her possessions as if to leave, and Helen sat down next to her.

"I'm going to set up an office somewhere because you're the third person to visit me here today," Megan confirmed.

"You must tell me what it's like to be so popular," Helen quizzed.

"Funnily enough, the previous person who you've just missed was your husband!" revealed Megan.

"I'm not surprised, but dare I ask what he wanted?"

"He was asking why I wasn't on an excursion today and about the party tonight."

"Oh, I thought it might have been something else. You see, this cruise is definitely a defining moment for Neil and I, and in that context, I am here to ask a favour of you?"

"I'm not sure I like the sound of this?" Megan replied hesitantly.

"Oh, this is good because you have a unique opportunity to have your cake and eat it."

"Go on..."

"I would like you to keep your eye on my husband and make sure he doesn't get led astray on this cruise."

Megan paused for a second.

"So, reading between the lines, you want me to 'flirt' with your husband?"

"In a manner of speaking, yes."

"And this will achieve what?"

"I'll find out for definite if my future is with Neil."

"And how far does flirting go exactly?"

"Make the first move and see how he reacts. He's all talk most of the time. He'll probably be so surprised, he'll run a mile!"

"And if he doesn't? Run a mile, I mean?"

"Then I'm trusting you to stop short."

"In going all the way?" Megan interrupted.

"Exactly, somehow I feel I can trust you and if I know he's with you, he can't be with anyone else."

"I don't make a habit of flirting with, or chasing for that matter, married men," Megan retorted.

"I'm sure you don't, but look on the plus side, here is a wife giving you permission beforehand!"

"I've not said yes yet, and I don't know if I feel comfortable with it."

"Think about it and see how tonight goes. I'm not planning on staying too late, so I might suggest to Louise we go to the casino."

"OK," Megan confirmed, a bit bewildered.

"Good, I'll see you later then?"

"Yes, fine, Helen."

By now, the sun decks were emptying and only the die-hard sun worshippers were remaining. Megan gathered her things and before she left, she noticed what looked like a business card underneath the sun lounger next to her. She picked it up to have a look and she saw it belonged to Rebecca. She must have dropped this earlier, although I don't know why she had it with her, Megan thought.

Rebecca Carebec, Cruise Reporter, Cruise News

Megan was intrigued by the card. I'll hang on to this and see what happens, she thought. Unusual name. She was contemplating the events of the afternoon, which was supposed to have been quiet and relaxing but instead, her friendship with Megan had grown; she was seemingly being admired by the handsome young man she had bumped into yesterday; and to top it all, she had been invited to flirt with Helen's husband, which was exactly what she had almost been doing anyway! The evening was going to be an eventful one.

CHAPTER 12 – BACK TO THE 80S

The Atlantic had left Bilbao behind and was cruising gently overnight towards Lisbon. The weather was warm and the sea calm, which would be perfect for the open deck party later that evening. If the previous night's dress code was black and white formal, then tonight couldn't be more different. Officially it was an 80s night, but there would also be a prize for the wildest T-shirt on view. Therefore, as the passengers arrived, there was a sea of colour on display as most of the passengers made a spirited effort to conform.

The centre stage was the 80s quiz and disco on the upper deck between the pool and Nevis's bar. Staff had been out late afternoon clearing the area. The chefs would be preparing food via a barbecue and Dave, the resident DJ, would be on hand at the disco and also on duty afterwards in the nightclub until the early hours. Elsewhere, the casino was having a 'fun' night with reduced minimum bets, and there were 80s shows in the theatre. It was going to be a fun and entertaining evening.

Henry and George were readying themselves for the 80s night. Their parents were going to attend the quiz and then move on to the theatre for the late show.

"Remember now, Henry, play it cool and be subtle," George reminded his big brother.

"The long game, I keep telling you, George, the long game."

The family made the short walk from their suite to the open deck area. The quiz was due to start at 9 p.m. sharp with the disco and barbecue at around 10p.m.

Rebecca called on Megan and the two of them made their way up together. Sarah and party, with Helen and Neil, completed the line-up, and by the time they all arrived, the deck was busy and lively with passengers ordering drinks and settling down for the quiz.

"Good evening, ladies and gentlemen. I'm Craig, your Cruise Director, and welcome to our 80s night. We'll shortly be starting the evening's proceedings with our 80s quiz, followed by the disco. There will be a barbecue later and, of course, plenty of drinks at Nevis's. There is also a prize for the most outrageous T-shirt and going by the colours before me, it isn't going to be easy to pick a winner! I'll hand you over to Sandra, who is going to be your quizmaster. I hope you all have a very enjoyable evening."

There were several teams for the quiz, which were restricted to a maximum of four per team, including Henry and family, Megan and Rebecca, Sarah and party, and Neil and Helen. Sandra made her introductions.

"Thank you, Craig. The quiz is to consist of twenty questions split into four sections: sport; music; films together with TV; and finally general knowledge. At the end of the quiz, can each team please pass their answers to the next team for marking? We also need a team name and the winners will receive a bottle of champagne. We'll start the quiz in around five minutes."

Rebecca had noticed two familiar faces at the other end of the deck area.

"Look, Megan, there's Henry and George with, I'm assuming, their parents."

"Oh god, I recognise them. I was sitting next to them both yesterday at Gavin's IT class!"

"Excellent, chasing the eldest son while giving the parents IT lessons, I like it," Rebecca teased.

"It's not funny and I've not told you what happened with Helen earlier yet."

"Intriguing, tell all!"

They were interrupted by Sandra.

"OK, we're about to start the quiz. We'll have a short gap between each section. First section is sport, so here goes. Question one. In 1986, Diego Maradona scored his now infamous 'Hand of God' goal against England. England lost that game with a score of 2-1, but who scored England's goal that night and also went on to win the Golden Boot for finishing top scorer in the tournament?"

The questions continued to flow, thick and fast.

"Moving on to music. What was the date of Live Aid in 1985?"

There were groans from some passengers.

"Come on, I never said they were going to be easy!" Sandra bellowed out.

"Finally, we move on to the general knowledge round. The stock market crash and the great storm that hit southern England both happened within a week of each other, but what month and year during the eighties did they both occur?" Sandra continued. "Does anyone want to hear any of the questions again?"

"Yes, but could you make them slightly easier this time?" remarked a passenger.

"I thought they were easy," Sandra replied. "OK, if that's everyone happy, please can you swap answer sheets between teams and we'll go through the answers shortly."

"So do tell all about Helen then?" quizzed Rebecca.

"Soon after her husband, Neil, paid me a visit, Helen came to ask me a favour."

"Go on," Rebecca asked in anticipation.

"It turns out Helen and Neil are having marital issues and this cruise is a bit of a make-or-break for them," Megan was now whispering.

"Has everyone swapped their answer sheets?" Sandra asked the passengers.

There was a chorus of agreement.

"OK, we'll start with the answers."

After around ten minutes, the score sheets were being passed back to their teams.

"Can you raise your hand if your team has scored 12 or more?"

A few hands were showing. Sandra continued towards 20 until only one hand was left.

"OK, we've reached 18 and we seem to have a winner. Give them a round of applause. Come on up and collect your champagne."

Two passengers moved towards Sandra, almost sheepishly.

"Is that the couple who you were sitting next to this afternoon on the other side of Henry and George?" Megan asked Rebecca.

"Yes, it is. How did they manage to score 18, that's not fair," Rebecca continued.

The couple collected their champagne and scurried back to their seats.

"OK, thank you to everyone who took part in the quiz. In about ten minutes or so, our resident DJ Dave is going to start our 80s disco. I'm reliably informed the barbecue is almost ready and, of course, Nevis's bar is open all night and our wonderful staff are waiting for you, so please enjoy your evening. Before I forget, for the next two hours or so up to midnight, to celebrate the 80s, all drinks will be 80 pence, so there is no excuse not to have a drink and enjoy yourselves."

There was much cheering from all the passengers.

Sandra moved towards Nevis's herself. The open deck was filling up as other passengers readied themselves for the disco, having missed the quiz.

"Anyway, you were saying?" quizzed Rebecca.

"You're not going to believe this but Helen asked me 'to keep an eye' on Neil."

"Oh, which means what exactly?"

"That's what I asked her because apparently, reading between the lines, he has a tendency to be a bit of a ladies' man. Anyway, she's left it open for me to flirt with Neil. Her thinking is, if I'm holding his attentions, he can't be chasing anyone else," Megan confirmed.

"OMG, you're joking!" Rebecca was almost shouting.

They both laughed together.

"What's so funny, Megan?" Sarah asked, having heard the commotions.

"Oh, just something from this afternoon," Megan replied.

"What are you going to do?" Rebecca whispered to Megan.

"Good evening, ladies and gentlemen. I hope you are all in the mood for some classic 80s tunes, mixed together with some modern songs, especially for the younger ones among you. I'm with you here for the next two hours or so, before we head off down to the nightclub until the early hours. Plenty to get through, so let's make a start." Dave was up and running, and as the first song blasted out, the dance floor area quickly filled.

"Boys, we are off to the theatre. Henry, I trust you will look after George. Enjoy yourselves and we'll see you tomorrow," Mary reminded them.

"Yes, thanks, see you tomorrow," came the reply in stereo.

Mary and John left the open deck and made their way towards the lifts.

"I've been looking at these cocktails, Henry, What do you think?"

"I think you should calm down. It's early."

"Where's your sense of adventure." George got the attentions of a waiter.

"'Sex on the beach' for me, thanks. Henry?"

"You're not having that!"

"Dare you? It's the closest you'll ever get to the real thing!"

"Oh, funny! I'll have a half lager to start, thanks," confirmed Henry to the waiter.

"Certainly, sir."

"Wow, pushing the boat out, aren't we? And no pun intended."

"I keep telling you, it's the long game, George. You've no idea."

Megan and Rebecca made their way across to Nevis's bar. Sarah and Paul were dancing on the deck, and Louise, Gavin, Helen and Neil were sitting together at the side. Dave was starting to warm up as the tunes passed one by one. One of the bar staff passed him a drink.

"This next song reminds me of a certain holiday years ago which I've not heard for a while, so let's play it now."

Sarah and Paul joined the others for a drink.

"I know where I remember Rebecca from now," Sarah exclaimed.

"Who's Rebecca?" asked Louise.

"Long story. I'll tell you later, Auntie."

"Believe me, it's a relief that she's remembered because it's driven me insane all afternoon," Paul confirmed, turning to Louise.

"Louise, do you fancy a few games of blackjack?" Helen asked.

"Try and stop me. Will you be alright, Gavin?"

"Of course. I need to speak to Craig about my next IT class. I'll pop down later to see how you're doing."

With that, Helen and Louise left to head down to the casino. To carry on the 80s theme, the casino's fun night was offering minimum bets at 80 pence on all tables until midnight. It was an opportunity not to be missed.

Back on deck, the drinks were taking their toll on some.

"How many have you had, George?"

"Not enough, Henry. Come on, join the party!"

"You're drunk, aren't you?"

"Am not!"

Henry started laughing. "OMG, my streetwise little brother has succumbed to cocktails!"

Dave the DJ started reminiscing.

"It was hot and sweaty that summer week, and I'm not just talking weather."

Rebecca and Megan were at Nevis's Bar but had been distracted by Dave's latest comment.

"That was a bit random from the DJ," Rebecca retorted. "Anyway, what are you going to do about Henry and Neil?"

"See what happens. Come on, let's have another drink."

Megan ordered for them both. George's earlier cocktails were kicking in, but this was only serving to make him even bolder than normal. On spotting Megan and Rebecca at the bar, he made his way across and stood next to them to order another drink. The bar was temporarily busy so he turned to Megan and got directly to the point.

"You know my brother fancies you, don't you?"

"Does he?" Megan answered, trying to keep a straight face. Rebecca burst out laughing.

"Did I say something funny?" George was slurring his words now.

Henry had noticed George at the bar and rushed across to join him. The barman was asking George what he wanted to drink.

"A large coke please, and another half lager for me, thanks," Henry instructed. "I must apologise for my brother's behaviour. I hope he hasn't offended you."

"Offended? I was making your introductions and setting you up," George replied.

"It's fine, really. I think he may have had one too many though," Megan teased slightly to Henry.

Dave continued his reminiscing.

"There was a build-up of heat and tension with an electric atmosphere."

Soon after Louise and Helen had left, Gavin spotted Craig and went to confirm the details for the second class, the day after tomorrow. Neil had moved towards the barbecue and ordered food, noticing how Megan was attracting attention. Sarah and Paul were left together.

"Have you noticed how close Megan and Rebecca have become, Paul?" Sarah asked.

"No, not really, and is it so bad?"

"I knew Rebecca's younger sister from school and didn't like her much."

"Maybe Rebecca's not like her sister," Paul pleaded.

"There's something not right about Rebecca and I'm going to find out what it is."

"If it makes you happy," Paul remarked with a sigh.

The barmen brought Henry and George their drinks. Megan spotted an easy opportunity and turned to Henry.

"George was saying you might want a dance?"

"Did he now!"

"Yes. So what do you say?" Megan pressed.

"Well, I'm not sure. I don't dance that well."

Megan nudged Henry towards the dancing area, holding his hand and leading the way.

"I need to sit down," George confirmed.

"Come on, over here, there's a table free." Rebecca helped George to sit down.

Helen and Louise had reached the casino and luckily found two seats together. Soon, Helen was opening up to Louise.

"You know this cruise is a bit of a make-or-break for Neil and myself."

"It's none of my business, Helen."

"How well do you know Megan?"

"What do you mean?"

"I sort of asked her a favour earlier today."

"Go on."

"I asked her to keep an eye on my husband for me."

"Oh, and what was her reaction?"

"I expected a lot worse! Are you OK with this?"

"She's my niece and I don't want her getting hurt but she's old enough to know for herself."

Megan and Henry had been dancing for a couple of songs and were feeling comfortable together. Dave was still reeling off the 80s songs but had been drinking what he thought were soft drinks. "This song I remember listening to when the ground moved for us both that week. In fact, I think for one of us, it was moving for the first time." Dave added to his earlier commentary.

Craig had been listening to Dave while talking to Gavin.

"Excuse me, Gavin. Give me a minute."

Craig moved towards Dave and sat him down.

"Sandra, take over for a while, will you?"

George was regretting the cocktails. All of a sudden, he felt rather sick. In a single moment that seemed to last forever, he had emptied the contents of his stomach all over the table and part of Rebecca's handbag. Henry had noticed the commotion and stopped dancing with Megan to rush across to help his brother.

"Ugh, thank you very much, George, I'm sure," screeched Rebecca.

"Aw, I feel awful."

"George, I told you about those cocktails. I'm so sorry," said Henry looking at Rebecca.

Megan couldn't stop laughing.

"I'm going to have to take my brother back to our suite and see how he is and try and cover for him from our parents in the morning."

"Thankfully, I have another handbag which I'm going to change now!" Rebecca shouted at the party before her.

Henry reluctantly left the disco and helped George back to their suite. A few crew members were on hand at once to clear up the mess. Sandra continued with the disco until midnight while Craig was investigating what Dave had been drinking. Gavin, Sarah and Paul left and headed for the casino to see how the others were faring. Megan had been left alone after Rebecca and the brothers' departures but this was only for a minute or two.

"So that was the competition?"

Neil had watched the commotion from the barbecue and now came across to where Megan was standing.

"I don't know what you mean."

"Pity he couldn't stay. Still, you're with the big boys now."

"Fancy yourself, don't you?"

"Yes, but I don't see you resisting."

Megan had enjoyed her dance with Henry, but as she had acknowledged before, there was a forbidden attraction to Neil and given Helen's instructions, she couldn't resist taking his advances further. It was shortly before midnight and Sandra was beginning to wind the disco down. There were quite a number of passengers on the dance floor, but Megan and Neil managed to find a place and joined in with a couple of group dances.

After a few slower songs to end the disco, Sandra confirmed that the winners of the wildest T-shirt would be announced in the sports bar next to the casino.

Megan walked hand in hand with Neil from the floor to Nevis's bar where they shared a joke and laughed together.

"Another drink?" she asked.

"Not really, but the night is still young."

They found a quiet corner of the deck and Megan started kissing Neil, who responded.

"I guess it's your place because it can't be mine?" Neil asked softly.

"Easy tiger, not on our first date?"

Megan led Neil towards the door into the inner decks. She kissed him again.

"See you tomorrow in Lisbon."

Neil tried to follow Megan through the door.

"Lisbon, tomorrow," Megan reiterated again, and left Neil at the door.

Rebecca had decided the incident with George and her handbag had been enough for the night and on her return to her cabin, she stayed there.

Megan walked back to her cabin with a wry smile on her face. Mission accomplished tonight, she thought, and still all to play for!

CHAPTER 13 – LISBON LIAISONS

Henry had risen early and after checking on George, who was fast asleep, he made his way downstairs to the living area of their suite. Both his parents were already up and admiring the view of Lisbon drawing nearer from the balcony.

"Good morning, Henry," his mother said reassuringly. "How was last night?"

"Fine, thanks."

"That doesn't sound very enthusiastic. Did you go anywhere after the disco?"

"No, we were both tired so we crashed back here afterwards." Henry wasn't giving anything away.

"I'm going for a walk to collect *the Daily News* and some Sudoku. Are you coming, Henry?" asked his father.

"Yes, why don't we can go on deck and watch Lisbon approaching?"

John and Henry's relationship had been strained over the years. John was a traditional father and did love his sons deep down, but unfortunately struggled to show it and it was often left to his wife Mary to carry the burden. However, Henry enjoyed being with his father. They shared many personality traits and joint interests, including a strong liking for puzzles and analytical problems.

The two of them strolled down to the library and collected a couple of Sudoku puzzles. They would have a competition later to see who could solve it first. As the sun was already streaming through from outside, they decided to go out and see what was going on. *The Atlantic* was continuing her slow passage towards its berth for the day. It slipped under the bridge beside the large Christ the King monument, which overlooks the city. Planes were flying overheard as they approached the airport. There were several passengers already admiring the view.

"Are you looking forward to your twenty-first, son?"

"Yes, I'm already enjoying this cruise. It will be good."

"We should have a special meal on Saturday, celebrate your birthday properly."

"That sounds good, and yours too?"

"Well, we'll see. You have your whole life to look forward to. I'm very proud of you in the way you've taken to joining the family business. It's a big relief for me knowing the business can safely be passed on when I retire."

"I know, Dad. I just hope I won't disappoint you."

"You'll never do that, Henry."

The two of them stopped and watched the scenery. It was a very relaxing moment for them both.

Neil had arrived back at their cabin first last night and was first to rise this morning. Like many others, he was admiring the view from their balcony. Helen rose soon afterwards.

"What did you get up to last night?" she asked.

"Oh, you missed all the fun. Some young lad was sick all over the table where Megan and her friend were sitting. It was quite amusing. Anyway, you came in after me. Did you win at blackjack?"

"I think I broke even and had a good chat with Louise."

"Yes, quite the new buddy all of a sudden, isn't she?"

"She's someone I can talk to, if that's what you mean."

There was a strange atmosphere. Helen had an idea what her husband was up to, but of course she wasn't letting on.

"Let's go upstairs for some breakfast before everyone else arrives," she confirmed.

Sarah had been thinking about Rebecca last night and what she might be up to. Knowing that Megan might have been told by

Rebecca how they knew of each other, she was dying to tell her younger cousin that she knew herself now. She made her way down to Megan's cabin and knocked on the door. Luckily Megan was up and preparing to leave for breakfast.

"Who is it?" she asked.

"Sarah."

There was a short delay before the door opened.

"Good morning, Megan. How are you today?" asked Sarah as she strolled into Megan's cabin.

"Have you swallowed a happy pill?"

"No, but I realised where I've met Rebecca from previously."

"Oh, that's good."

"Depends, but it was her younger sister that I knew. She was in my class at school. I'm sure I met Rebecca at least once during that time. From memory, I didn't like her younger sister much."

"In my experience, younger sisters are alright," remarked Megan, with a hint of sarcasm.

Megan was scurrying around getting ready and Sarah was an annoying distraction. Sarah moved towards the table and noticed a business card. On closer inspection, it was Rebecca's. Carefully checking that Megan wasn't looking, she picked it up and hid it in her pocket.

"I trust we're going up for breakfast with the others and you're not just checking on my welfare, or Rebecca's for that matter?"

Sarah, now smiling slightly, replied, "Of course, dear cousin, if you're ready?"

Megan opened the door and followed Sarah out as they made their way to breakfast.

Helen and Neil were making their way back from breakfast but on their return, their cabin hadn't been attended to. The Cabin Steward was running late.

"Are we going to have to wait in the corridor now?" Neil asked, turning to Helen.

"Yes, but I'm sure we won't have to wait long."

"It's a bit inconvenient," he continued.

Austin, their Cabin Steward, had just started on their cabin.

"Good morning, sir, madam. How are you today?"

"We're fine, thanks, Austin. Running a bit late?" Helen asked politely.

"Yes, sorry, madam. I'll be finished shortly."

"Yes, you will, but not just our cabin!" Neil barked out loud.

Austin scampered inside. Neil's raised voice had attracted the attention of Austin's manager, who was nearby

"Can I help you at all, madam, sir?" he asked as he approached them both.

"Our cabin isn't ready yet!" bellowed Neil.

"Neil, would you please stop shouting, it isn't helping! It's fine, honestly," Helen continued, turning to the smartly dressed cabin manager.

"No problem, madam. I'll have a word with Austin when he's finished his shift this morning."

"There is no need for that and I'll be annoyed if you do!" Helen confirmed.

"OK, madam, if you're sure?"

"Quite, thank you."

Austin, who had heard the entire conversation, came out of their cabin and stood beside Helen. His manager was talking to Neil further along the corridor.

"Thank you very much, madam, it won't happen again," he said softly.

"It's alright, Austin, don't worry. You'll tell me if your manager has words with you later, won't you?"

Austin smiled and moved along to the next cabin. His manager said his goodbyes to Neil and started talking to Austin.

As with Bilbao, many passengers were taking the opportunity to explore Lisbon and the surrounding area. The weather was hot and sunny, and with a full day here, there was plenty of opportunity for everyone to see the sights. Gavin, Louise and Megan had booked the jeep safari, Sarah and Paul were going on a walking tour of the city, Helen and Neil had opted for the Oceanarium, and Henry, George and their parents were taking in the sights by coach with a visit to the cathedral and museum.

Gavin and Louise hadn't seen much of their niece since they boarded and the jeep safari was going to give them an opportunity to catch up with her. There were six passengers in each jeep and they would be away until mid-afternoon.

"I was having a chat with Helen last night at the casino," Louise said, turning to Megan.

"Oh, that was nice. Did you win?"

"She said she had a chat with you earlier yesterday afternoon."

"Yes, she did pop by, while I was sunbathing."

"She mentioned the favour she asked of you."

"Right, how was she about it?" Megan asked her aunt.

"Never mind her, how do you feel?"

"I was a bit surprised, I must confess."

"I don't want you to get hurt or involved, Megan."

"No one's going to get hurt."

"You can guarantee that, can you?"

"No, but it's on my terms, and anyway, it's a bit of fun."

Louise raised her eyebrow and turned to Gavin. "Oh, I'm staying well out of this one, Louise," he said.

"I'm not happy about it, Megan. Did anything happen last night with Neil?"

"No, not really. Something funny did happen though. The younger brother of someone I was dancing with was sick all over a table and it caught part of Rebecca's handbag. She wasn't pleased at all!"

"Is that Rebecca who was helping you with the quiz last night?" Gavin asked.

"Yes, she was, and I thought we were going to win."

One of the passengers asked Megan a question, which distracted her for a while.

"Did you notice what Megan was doing after I left, Gavin?" asked Louise to her husband.

"Afraid not, I was talking to Craig about my class tomorrow."

"Oh, men! You're useless!"

Sarah and Paul had decided to spend some time together on a walking tour around Lisbon's narrow streets and city sights. It was relaxed and romantic as they strolled around hand in hand together.

"Paul, you know how I said I was going to find out about Rebecca?"

"Yes," Paul said hesitantly.

"Well, when I was in Megan's cabin this morning, there was a business card of hers on the table, so I grabbed it when she wasn't looking."

"Dare I ask?"

"Apparently she's a cruise reporter for a magazine."

"There you go then, perfectly innocent."

"I'm certain there's more to it than that!"

"I'm not spending this entire cruise 'goose-chasing'!"

"Bear with me, Paul. I'll make it worth your while."

Sarah pulled Paul towards her and they shared a kiss on the corner of a cobbled narrow street.

When George finally awoke, his head was thumping and the last thing he wanted was to step outside his bed. Henry and his father returned together, but by now his mother, Mary, knew something wasn't right.

"I thought I asked you to look after your younger brother? Why is he not well? He's nursing a hangover; what on earth was he drinking?"

"He may have had the odd cocktail."

"I left him in your hands, you shouldn't have let him have cocktails; he's only sixteen!"

"I suspect he's going to suffer for it today."

Henry ran up the stairs to their bedroom. George was still moving around gingerly.

"Thank you for last night, by the way. I just needed a younger brother being sick at that precise moment."

"I'm not going to make it easy for you, big brother. Anyway, I think I'm paying for it now."

"Good, hopefully it will teach you a lesson."

Their mother called them down as their excursion was starting soon. It was going to be a long day for George.

By mid-afternoon, most of the half-day excursions were finished and several passengers had elected to stay in Lisbon for the afternoon to explore. The open-top buses were popular because it is a good way to see the city views and landmarks.

Sarah and Paul had arranged to meet the others on one of those buses and all five decided to sit upstairs in the sunshine. Gavin and Louise sat together, as did Sarah and Paul but across the aisle. Megan sat just in front of her aunt and uncle. Lisbon was busy this afternoon and the traffic was crawling through the streets. The tour was set to last an hour, but given the traffic it was going to take much longer. A few stops later, a familiar couple arrived and grabbed the last two seats, one beside Megan and the other one next to another passenger in front of Sarah and Paul.

"Fancy meeting you all here," Helen remarked.

"Did you enjoy the aquarium?" Louise asked.

"Yes, it was OK, thanks. Nice to have a few hours away from the ship."

Helen, who had sat in front of Sarah and Paul, started fishing.

"Did you guys enjoy the disco after Louise and I left last night?"

"Yes, thanks, we did, but we left shortly afterwards," confirmed Sarah.

"Megan, am I right in saying your friend had an unfortunate incident with her handbag?"

"A teenage boy was sick all over the table and caught part of it."

"Was he with anyone?" Helen continued.

"His older brother took him back to their, suite I think," Megan's response was cautious and non-committal.

"Were you with them, Megan?"

Neil, who had been forced to sit beside Megan by Helen's strategic choice of seat, looked at Megan with a hint of annoyance, even slight anger.

"The younger brother joined Rebecca and I at the bar, but I think he had too much to drink."

Rebecca's day started in a very relaxed way because she decided to stay on board *the Atlantic* in the morning, not venturing out until after lunch. She took one of the many shuttle buses that CZN provide for their passengers into Lisbon and boarded a city tour bus. Like the others, it was very busy but she managed to find a single seat upstairs. There were a few bus companies operating these for the tourists and occasionally they would pull alongside each other. The traffic lights had gone red and there was a long queue waiting.

"Speaking of Rebecca, isn't that her there on the bus next to us?" asked Sarah, who had a good view on her side of the bus.

"I think so, but I can't really see her clearly," replied Megan.

Sarah started to wave at Rebecca, who acknowledged her with a smile.

"You didn't arrange to see Rebecca today, Megan?" asked Sarah again.

"No, I haven't seen her since last night."

The two buses went their separate ways. It was late afternoon and although the ship wasn't due to leave for another couple of hours, the parties decided to catch a shuttle bus back to *the Atlantic*. At the pick-up point, there was a large queue of passengers now and Helen, Neil, Sarah and Paul boarded one bus, while Louise, Gavin and Megan waited for the next one. Unknown to Megan, Henry, George and their parents were further down the queue and would make it onto the next shuttle bus. Once Megan had sat down in her seat, she noticed the two brothers but there was nothing she could do. As they approached the ship, she had an idea. The family were one of the first to leave the bus but Henry deliberately walked quite slowly, allowing Megan to catch them up.

"How's George been today?" Megan asked enthusiastically towards Henry.

"In the dog house, and reeling from a hangover."

"Oh, hello, it's Megan isn't it? Your uncle took the IT class the other day," interrupted Mary.

Megan was somewhat taken aback.

"Oh yes, you remembered."

"Why wouldn't I? Your uncle's class was very helpful and, as I recall, so were you in helping my husband and I."

Henry and Megan shared a smile.

"Will you be at his class tomorrow?" Mary continued.

Gavin and Louise had caught up with Megan and the family party as they continued the walk towards *the Atlantic*.

"I'm glad you enjoyed my class, madam," said Gavin, in a posh tone.

Gavin's intervention surprised Mary completely.

"Oh yes, I did, thanks, and we're both looking forward to tomorrow's class."

"Excellent, we'll see you there."

Gavin and Louise had now passed the family and Megan and joined the queue to board *the Atlantic*. Megan and Henry had fallen slightly behind the others.

"Are you attending the class tomorrow?" Henry whispered.

"I will be unless I have a better offer?"

Henry went a shade of red. George had fallen behind his parents and had joined Megan and Henry.

"In other words, big brother, make her an offer!"

"You know the champagne bar on the upper deck?" blurted Henry.

"I think so."

"Meet me there around 2 p.m. tomorrow afternoon?"

"OK, but what about your parents?"

"Hopefully they should be at your uncle's class."

They all passed through security and made their separate ways towards their accommodation on board.

"Nice girl, that Megan," commented Mary, as they reached their suite.

"Yes, she seems to be."

"It's D-day tomorrow, then, big brother!"

Louise, Gavin and Megan stopped at the lifts. Louise was looking for answers.

"Were you with that young man last night?"

"As I said, his younger brother was sick over the table next to Rebecca."

"Yes, I know all that."

Megan started smiling.

"You were, weren't you?"

"Good for you!" Gavin shouted enthusiastically.

"Do you not remember what was discussed earlier?"

"Is there a problem with Megan?"

The lift doors opened and Louise and Gavin stepped inside.

Megan's cabin was only a couple of decks up.

"I'll walk from here," she confirmed.

"And I'll speak to you later, young lady," Louise confirmed as the doors closed.

"Not a word, Gavin, not a word."

Gavin looked rather perplexed as the lift ascended the decks. Megan walked towards her cabin with another wry smile. Events were beginning to fall into place rather well.

CHAPTER 14 – STORMY SEAS

When *the Atlantic* slipped the docks and left Lisbon, the Captain made the following announcement.

"Good evening, ladies and gentlemen, I hope you had a lovely day with us in Lisbon. I have mentioned to you previously about an ex-hurricane in the Atlantic Ocean this week, and it is time to update you now. The latest weather reports confirm the storm is weakening but taking a more northerly course than was first thought. We are, however, anticipating some rough seas and fairly high swells tomorrow morning and into the early afternoon, as the storm tracks north-eastwards.

"As a result, we will be taking a slightly more coastal route when we cross the Bay of Biscay tomorrow. As a precaution, all outside decks will be closed from midnight tonight and the swimming pools on the upper decks will remain closed until further notice. When moving around the ship tomorrow, please take extra care and use the handrails on the stairs. This ship has been built to withstand storms more powerful than the one we are expecting tomorrow and I am very confident we will sail through to quieter waters tomorrow afternoon. That said, I hope you enjoy your evening with us on board *the Atlantic* and a further update will be relayed to you tomorrow morning."

There was an uneasy atmosphere on board *the Atlantic* during the evening. Many passengers decided on an early night, in the hope of catching some quality sleep before the storm took hold in the morning. A few passengers were still playing at the casino, but most of the bars were quiet and the nightclub was closed.

It had been a busy night on the bridge for the Captain and his officers. Regular weather updates were monitored and analysed as *the Atlantic* sailed towards the bay overnight, keeping as close to the coast as possible. By 7 a.m., the storm was passing close by and the swell outside was increasing. An hour later, the Captain was on the tannoy again.

"Good morning, ladies and gentlemen. This is your Captain speaking with an update on the weather. The storm's strength and projected course have not changed since last night, but as you have probably noticed, there is a large swell beneath us. We anticipate the effect of the storm to peak in the next few hours before slowly receding early afternoon. My message to you hasn't changed since last night. Please remember to take extra care when walking inside the ship and use the handrails on the stairs. I will give you a further update at midday."

Sarah and her family group had decided to have a buffet breakfast on the upper deck then all meet for a coffee in the bar. In hand was a copy of *the News* telling passengers what activities were scheduled today. Given the weather and the fact that most of the outside decks were closed, additional entertainment had been provided on the inner decks.

"What are we doing today, guys?" Louise started the conversation.

"Remember I have to see Craig soon to finalise this afternoon's class."

"You're even in *the News*, Uncle. 'IT class for beginners, part two at 2 p.m.' Paul and I are going to the library first, though."

"You're going to the library?" Megan asked sarcastically.

The storm was beginning to take hold. Some lights flickered on and off. A crew member was finishing hoovering the floors.

"Only on a cruise will you find staff continuously working, even in the face of adversity," Louise commented.

The lights flickered again and a book dropped to the floor, which startled some passengers.

"Here we go, hold on to your hats, everyone!" Gavin confirmed as he looked outside to see the sea swell and the ship tilt slightly.

"Yes, the library, if that's OK with you!"

Megan simply shrugged her shoulders.

"Anyway, young lady, you're coming shopping with me!" Louise bellowed at Megan.

Having elected to have breakfast in their suite, Henry, George and their parents were preparing to go their separate ways. Mary and John were going to seek refuge in the cinema with a classic movie and ride the worst of the storm out, while George was going to spend time in the older teenagers' club playing video games.

"What are you going to do this morning, Henry?" his mother asked.

"I might have a look at this storm, see how high the swell goes, then I've noticed there's a Battle of the Sexes Quiz in the sports bar later."

"Come to the IT class with us this afternoon, son. That nice girl we met yesterday will be there because it's her uncle taking it."

"Might do, enjoy the film. I'll see you later."

Henry left their suite and sauntered down the corridor, holding on to the railings as the ship battled through the storm. He had a few hours to kill before his arranged meeting with Megan and therefore had no intention of any IT class later. With no better ideas, he walked up to the library for some reading.

"Let's all meet back in the sports bar for the Battle of the Sexes Quiz, which shouldn't be a problem for us girls to win," Louise suggested.

"Sounds like a challenge. Are you up for this, Paul?" asked Gavin.

"Assuming I can drag Sarah away from the library, yes, it certainly does."

"Right, see everyone later." Louise rose first with Megan following close behind.

Louise was almost marching along the corridor towards the shops. Megan knew that a talking to was coming.

"What are you doing flirting with two men, one of who is married, in case you had forgotten?"

"I seem to remember being asked to flirt by the wife."

"Helen is going through a rough patch with her marriage and is probably rather vulnerable at the moment. I don't want you taking advantage."

They reached the shops and started browsing together. There was an uneasy silence.

"Are you coming to Gavin's class later?"

"No, I have a hot date with Neil." Megan smiled at her aunt who smirked back.

"It's not funny, Megan. I don't want you getting involved."

"It's under control, really it is."

"Dare I ask who you'll be with later? Actually don't tell me, I'd rather not know," Louise said with a resigned tone in her voice.

The atmosphere between them changed, and aunt and niece started laughing together at the situation. A familiar face appeared in the shop, which improved things further.

"Looking for a new handbag?" Megan asked as Rebecca appeared before her.

"Very funny. Anyway, what's happening with you?"

Fancy a coffee? And I'll tell all and you can tell me what you're really doing on board? I found a business card of yours the other day and now I can't find it, but I think Sarah might have it. And oh, she remembers where she's seen you from!"

"Lot's to catch up with then. Coffee it is."

"Are you coming, Louise?"

"No, you go with Rebecca and I'll see you later."

Gavin and Craig were talking near the atrium. The ship was still rocking up and down in the swell. Every now and again, a glass fell and smashed, or a passenger lost their balance. With the outside decks closed, the ship felt busy inside and the storm was the topic of conversation with all the passengers.

"Have you experienced anything like this before, Craig?"

"Yes, en route to Greenland was memorable for the storm we sailed through, it was worse than this. The Captain knows what he's doing, and by this afternoon we'll be fine."

"What are your thoughts on this afternoon's class?"

"I suspect, given the weather, the class will be very busy. We've included it in *the News* and they'll be another tannoy announcement after midday. The class is due to start around 2 p.m. in the same place as before and if you continue where you left off and take it a step further, with more advanced features of emails, spreadsheets, that kind of thing. Thirty to forty-five minutes should be enough, but you can extend it to about an hour if you feel you need to."

"I must admit, I enjoyed taking the class the other day."

"Good, and the feedback I received was very positive from the passengers, so a big thank you again, Gavin, for stepping in at the last minute for us. I will be there to introduce you and will stay for the duration this time."

"No pressure, then!"

"You'll be fine."

Sarah and Paul reached the library. There was a purpose about Sarah that Paul hadn't seen before, as if Rebecca had given her something to get her teeth into. The library was next door to the cyber study. The two of them approached the crew member at the desk.

"Do we need to open an account to use the internet?" Sarah asked.

"No, madam, only if you want to send and receive emails. We do make a small charge to your cabin number for internet use, though."

"That's fine, can we use the internet now, please?"

The cyber study wasn't normally the busiest place on the ship, however today was an exception. All the PCs were in use, but luckily another passenger was leaving and Sarah and Paul were directed to sit there.

"Right, let's have a look at this Cruise Reporter for Cruise News. I bet there is no such magazine!" Sarah remarked.

"I don't know what you're hoping to find?"

"I don't think Rebecca is a Cruise Reporter, but I'd like to find out what she is doing."

"Remember, we're supposed to be on holiday?"

"This won't take long. After this, we'll go down to the Battle of the Sexes Quiz."

"Hurrah to that," Paul confirmed.

Craig and Sandra would be hosting the Battle of the Sexes Quiz in the sports bar, which was already filling up when they arrived. The bar was splitting into two sections, males to one side and females the other. Gavin, Paul and Neil were sitting together, and on the other side Megan and Rebecca were together with Sarah, Louise and Helen sitting at another table.

"This is going to be a busy quiz today, Sandra. I hope you're ready for a defeat."

"May I remind you the girls are ahead in this competition since we started it!"

Craig was checking the equipment with the maintenance crew while Sandra ordered drinks for them both. The ship was under the influence of the storm and everyone was moving slowly and carefully to the tables and chairs to sit down.

"Good morning, ladies and gentlemen, and welcome to the Battle of the Sexes Quiz, one in which the guys are going to win today, right?"

There was a huge cheer from one half of the bar.

"We'll get started in a minute or two, and I'll leave Sandra to explain the format."

As Sandra was walking across to Craig with the drinks in the girl's part of the bar, the ship rocked slightly and she lost her balance. Both Cokes flew out of the glasses and onto the floor. Luckily they didn't land on any passengers. There were huge cheers from the guys and banter back from the girls' side.

"Come on, Sandra, I'll get the drinks, you make a start," reassured Craig.

"Right, that's today's deliberate mistake, now on with the quiz. Come on, girls, don't let me down! There will be ten general knowledge questions open to the whole bar. I need each team to nominate a Captain and after each question, someone needs to bring a written answer to either Craig or myself. In the event of a tie, we will keep going until there is a winner."

For the next half an hour, there was much banter and laughter as the passengers almost forgot what was happening outside.

By the time Henry arrived, the bar was packed and the quiz well underway. He sneaked in almost unnoticed and sat at the bar.

"Right, the scores are eight all and we therefore have a tie. We will keep going until one side doesn't answer correctly. To make it more interesting, each side picks the topic of the question the other side has to answer. Ladies first, I think, so guys, pick a topic for the girls' question, please"

The atmosphere was loud and joyful, but then a touch of reality kicked in when the bell rang, the clocks struck midday and an announcement came from the Bridge.

"Good afternoon, ladies and gentlemen, the time is 12 noon

and this is your Captain speaking from the Bridge. *The Atlantic* has continued her slightly more coastal route through the bay this morning because the storm has passed us to the north-west. I am happy to report the worst of the storm is behind us now and the swell and wind speed should start to recede in the next few hours. The outside decks and swimming pools will remain closed this afternoon, and please continue to take extra care in the corridors and public areas.

"Tonight's dress code has been changed to smart casual. *The Atlantic* has navigated the storm well, as we thought she might. Please enjoy your afternoon with us on board, ladies and gentlemen. Bear with the storm for a few more hours or so, because the weather forecast for the remainder of the cruise is warm, dry and sunny."

There was a huge cheer from within the sports bar. Craig made an announcement.

"You heard the Captain, ladies and gentlemen, so on with winning the quiz!"

Sandra grabbed the microphone from Craig.

"Right then, guys, what is the topic of the question for the girls?"

"Cricket!"

There was much shouting back and general groans.

"Cricket it is then," Sandra confirmed.

Craig asked the question, which was now open to anyone in the bar. No one answered so the question was now for the guys.

"Girls, what are we picking for the guys?" Sandra bellowed out.

"Greek mythology!"

There was huge laughter.

"Excellent, here we go then," Sandra enthused.

The question was asked and as before, ten seconds was allowed for the answer. The Captain of the male team made a last-minute plea.

"Any ideas anyone, please? Come on, we don't want the girls to beat us, do we?"

Suddenly an answer was forthcoming. The whole bar fell silent and everyone looked across to see who had blurted it out.

"Just repeat that for us, lad," the team Captain said.

Henry, now blushing slightly, confirmed his initial answer.

"That will do for me, are we right?" asked the Captain, standing up from his seat.

Sandra looked in disbelief as she had the answer in front of her. Craig knew it as well and jumped in quickly, shouting, "I think we have a winner!"

The guys erupted in celebration and were dancing around the floor. There was stone silence from the girls in complete disbelief and bewilderment. The answer had someone's praise though.

"Not only drop-dead gorgeous, but clever as well," Rebecca whispered to Megan.

Megan just smiled back while looking across to see Henry. Her view was blocked because several of the guys had surrounded him in celebration and were offering any drink he fancied from the bar.

"Lunch before Gavin's class, I think," Louise said despondently.

The bar started to empty slightly as everyone gathered their thoughts after the events of the quiz and decided what they would be going to next. There was to be a band appearing next in the sports bar because the CZN staff had increased the inside entertainment on offer due to the storm. Having calmed down, Gavin, Paul and Neil joined up with their respective partners and headed for lunch.

"Is Megan not joining us for lunch?"

"No, Gavin, I think she has plans this afternoon," confirmed Louise.

Megan and Rebecca stayed in the sports bar and grabbed a

sandwich together. Henry was totally embarrassed with all the attention and after being almost caressed into accepting a drink, elected for a half lager before slipping away again.

The Midnight Jets were setting up for their performance as Megan and Rebecca sat in each other's company. The atmosphere was relaxed, thanks to the Captain's announcement, which had reassured the passengers there was light at the end of the tunnel and the storm was almost done with.

"Good afternoon, my name is Suzanne. We are the Midnight Jets, and for the next half an hour we will be distracting you from what is happening outside, with several cool tunes to enjoy."

In perfect timing, an empty chair rolled across the floor as the ship swayed up and down and from side to side. Suzanne's stand also fell and some plates smashed behind the bar. It was a bizarre scene.

"I can see that some songs might be more difficult than I thought," Suzanne continued laughing.

Rebecca and Megan stayed and enjoyed the music together, and after Suzanne and her band had finished, Rebecca left Megan alone, while she contemplated her drinks with Henry.

CHAPTER 15 – AFTERNOON ADVENTURES

John and Mary were looking forward to the IT class because they had found Gavin's first class informative and educational. After the cinema in the morning, a buffet lunch followed, before they made their way to the classroom. On arrival, Gavin was there to greet them.

"Hello, I'm glad you could make it today. Please take a seat inside."

"Thank you. Is your lovely niece here today?" Mary asked.

"Megan? No, she has other plans this afternoon, apparently."

"Oh, that's a shame, she was so helpful last time."

Other passengers were queuing behind them as John and Mary entered the room.

"Where is Megan this afternoon?" Gavin asked Louise.

"Believe me, you don't want to know!"

As anticipated by Craig earlier, there were far more passengers today than before and the room was full to bursting. In attendance, of course, were Sarah, Paul, Helen and Neil, as well as a large number of new faces. As before, Louise was at the front ready to assist Gavin when needed. Craig made his introductions.

"Good afternoon, ladies and gentlemen, and welcome to the second of our IT classes for beginners, which has very kindly been taken by one of our passengers, Gavin. I see the room is full today, and I'm sure Gavin won't mind me saying the weather may have enticed many of you here today. This is actually a follow-up class from Monday's introduction and is due to last about forty-five minutes to an hour. So without further ado, I'll hand you to Gavin."

Henry had reached the champagne bar early, and was feeling extremely nervous and way out of his comfort zone. He quickly ordered a glass of champagne for Dutch courage and settled down at the bar, watching the swell of the sea outside. CZN had introduced limited exclusivity for loyal passengers, and the champagne bar, at certain times of the day, was one example.

Megan had stayed in the sports bar until almost 2 p.m. Feeling slightly nervous herself, she made her way towards the champagne bar, but was stopped by an officer at the entrance.

"I'm sorry, madam, this bar is only open to certain members this afternoon."

"Oh, I've arranged to meet someone here," Megan replied, with a hint of disappointment in her response.

Henry had noticed Megan and walked towards her.

"She's with me," he said, as he produced his membership card.

The officer looked at Henry's card. "Oh, that's fine, sir. Please, madam, come in."

Megan looked at the officer and gave him a polite smile. Henry led Megan in.

"I had forgotten about the member's club. I'm sorry, I should have met you at the entrance."

"Don't worry, I'm here now," reassured Megan.

"What would you like to drink?"

"I'll have a champagne, thanks."

They stood at the bar but didn't have to wait long for Megan's champagne arrived.

"You certainly know your Greek mythology."

Henry's face went red. "Oh, it was nothing really. Would you like a seat away from the window?"

"Yes, thanks, if possible. Do you mind the storm?"

"No, not really, I've sailed quite a bit over the years, with my family."

They moved across to a table near the entrance, far away from the window and the rough sea view.

Megan stumbled slightly as the ship swayed in the swell. "Whoops, I think I'm supposed to do this after a few drinks."

They both laughed. The mood was relaxed and the ice had definitely been broken, quite naturally by the situation they found themselves in together.

Back in the IT classroom, Gavin looked at the crowd of passengers in front of him in the room.

"Many thanks, Craig. Good afternoon, ladies and gentlemen. Today's class, as Craig mentioned is a step up from Monday's session. Due to the numbers today, you are going to have to share the PCs between yourselves. Louise is here to assist you and we're both here to answer any questions, along with Craig, of course. Right, let's get started."

After a drink or two in the champagne bar, Henry and Megan were very much enjoying each other's company. The bar was quiet, the storm was beginning to lose its influence, and the atmosphere was relaxed.

"Lovely though this is, I can't spend all afternoon sipping champagne," said Megan, opening up the opportunities.

"No, I suppose we can't, however, I have sort of arranged something," Henry blurted out.

"Sounds intriguing."

"Come with me." Henry's champagne was just about keeping him together.

Henry led Megan out of the bar. Megan grabbed his hand as they walked together away from the bar.

George had a very enjoyable morning at the teenagers' club. Every child was seemingly here today, given the storm outside.

The suggested itinerary had been changed and a video games competition was planned this afternoon.

John and Mary were struggling slightly with the IT class this afternoon. Louise was at hand to assist them.

"It's a pity Megan isn't here. She was so helpful last time," Mary groaned.

"Yes, she is good when she puts her mind to it."

"Do you know where she is?"

Louise tried hard to keep a straight face. She had a good idea.

"No, I'm afraid I don't."

"Well, tell her she was sadly missed, won't you?"

"I'll pass it on, yes."

Henry and Megan arrived at Henry's family suite. They went inside.

"Please make yourself comfortable," Henry said as he wandered across to the balcony.

"You're full of surprises, aren't you?" Megan replied in a soft tone.

There was a knock at the door.

"Ah, just in time," Henry went to the door, had a peek at who was outside and opened it.

"Room service, sir," confirmed the waiter.

"Yes, certainly, thanks, please bring it inside."

The waiter carried a tray inside with strawberries, two glasses and a bottle of champagne.

"Where would you like me to put the tray down, sir?"

"On the table on the balcony, thanks."

The waiter carefully placed the tray as instructed.

"Thank you very much."

"Have a pleasant afternoon, sir, madam."

"Yes, we will, thank you."

The waiter left, leaving them together.

"Your room service awaits, madam." Henry showed Megan to her seat.

"What about the storm? I'm going to feel a bit exposed," Megan hesitated slightly.

"It's moving away from us now. The swell is down and the wind much lighter than what it was. You'll be fine, trust me."

Megan sat herself down as she looked outside at a fairly angry sea. At least that's what she thought. Henry popped open the bottle. It startled Megan.

"Have some of this. It will calm us down."

"I'm the one that's feeling nervous," Megan retorted.

Henry was more nervous than he could ever remember. He passed the strawberries to Megan.

"Have a strawberry. They go with the champers rather well."

Megan picked up a couple of strawberries. They sat on the balcony watching the sea roll by together. The suite was on the upper deck, which was well away from the now receding swell of the sea below. The champagne was helping with both of their respective nerves but in completely different ways. This moment together could have lasted forever.

Suddenly, there was a sound at the cabin door, but not a knock. Someone was coming in. Henry bolted from his chair and pushed Megan towards the edge of the balcony, out of view from the door.

"Quick, come here," he shouted.

Megan, almost falling over, was bundled towards the corner of the balcony. Henry peered from her side to see who was coming in.

George opened the door and entered the suite. After a minute or two, he noticed the champagne bottle and two glasses on the balcony.

"Oh, it's only you!" Henry shouted at George.

"Entertaining, are we? Our parents are going to love this."

"Our parents aren't going to find out, are they?"

Megan came into view for George.

"Hello, Megan, I hope you're not leading Henry astray?"

"Rebecca says hello and is looking for a new handbag, if you're interested."

"Touché, I think! No time to waste, I'll leave you two lovebirds to it. Don't do anything I wouldn't do, will you, Henry? I know that will be difficult for you!"

"Goodbye, George! Enjoy your kiddies' activities, won't you?"

George left the suite. Henry and Megan burst into laughter.

"That was too close for comfort. Come on, we better clear the table and tidy up," Henry said turning to Megan.

"I haven't had the tour yet, what's upstairs?"

"Once we've tidied up here first."

They quickly finished the champagne and tidied what they could. Megan took Henry's hand and started ascending the stairs. She stopped near the top and turned to face Henry. She pulled him towards her and they shared a passionate kiss. Just as they were about to move up the remaining stairs, a familiar noise came from downstairs. Voices could be heard and the door started to open again.

"That was a good IT class this afternoon John, even though that lovely young girl, Megan, wasn't there this time."

Megan was about to splutter with laughter, but Henry covered her mouth with his hand. They very quickly crept upstairs and into Henry's bedroom.

"Wait there," whispered Henry.

"What am I going to do?" Megan replied, now panicking.

"Leave it to me."

Henry steadied himself and walked back down the stairs. His parents were still chatting about the class.

"IT class finished? Was it good?"

"Yes, it was, thanks. What are you up to?" his mother asked.

"Oh, nothing, just a quiet drink on the balcony. You've just missed George."

"Have we? Oh, that was a shame. What's he doing now?" Mary asked.

"I think he's playing video games." Henry was all over the place and feeling very stressed.

"I see the storm's receding, Henry. Do you remember that one we experienced in the English Channel a couple of years back?" his father asked.

"Hmm, yes, I think so."

"Are you OK, son? You look like you've seen a ghost," remarked his mother.

Henry whispered to himself that he wished he had.

"Yes, I'm fine. Why don't you change and I'll make us all a coffee?"

"Good idea. We can sit on the balcony and watch the storm," his father confirmed enthusiastically.

Henry was in a time warp. Megan was as silent as a mouse upstairs. As his parent's ascended the stairs, Henry put the kettle on, which he thought might help in blocking out any unwanted noises.

Megan heard both of them pass by Henry's bedroom and peered round the door to see them entering their bedroom. She looked downstairs to see Henry waving her down.

As the kettle was in full flow, she very carefully descended the stairs and was escorted to the door by Henry. They shared a quick kiss together before Henry opened the door and let Megan out.

Gavin and Louise were finishing tidying up the room, having seen all the passengers leave the class.

"I think that went very well, Gavin," Craig confirmed.

"Yes, I enjoyed that better today, even though there were more passengers in attendance."

"I wonder how Megan is getting on?" Louise asked.

"What are you not telling me?"

"Have you not worked it out yet?"

"I think I'll leave you two to it then?" Craig confirmed, noticing a possible domestic situation emerging.

"Yes, that's fine, Craig, thanks," Gavin turned as Craig walked out of the room.

"You mean Megan and the son of the older couple who were asking about her?"

Yes, exactly, the penny has dropped. Men, you know nothing!"

16 – EVENING ENTERTAINMENT

Before the sittings for dinner, there was by now a familiar announcement on the tannoy.

"Good evening, ladies and gentlemen, this is your Captain speaking, with a final storm update for you. I am pleased to report the storm has continued its north-easterly track away from our position and course. The seas and resulting swell we are experiencing have greatly reduced in the last few hours, and will continue to ease this evening. The outside decks are now open to all passengers, but the pools will remain closed until tomorrow. Our ship, *the Atlantic*, is in fine shape, so it just leaves me to wish you a very pleasant evening on board with us at CZN Cruises."

Sarah and her family group were sitting in the bar after dinner. Megan had yet to arrive.

"I wanted to show you this business card I found the other day, Gavin," Sarah said innocently.

"OK, whose is it?"

Sarah passed the card to her uncle.

"Rebecca Carebec. Is that not who Megan has befriended?"

"Let's have a look, Gavin?" Louise asked.

Gavin passed it to Louise.

"There's something not right about her, Paul and I searched the internet earlier, but came up with nothing."

"Why do you think there's something unusual, Sarah? Megan seems to be friendly with her?" Louise quizzed.

"Don't encourage her, she's driving me to distraction," Paul sighed.

"The defence rests its case," Sarah confirmed.

"Sarah?" Louise scowled at her.

"I'll tell you one thing that might be classed as unusual," Gavin said. "Have you looked at her name?"

"Rebecca Carebec?" Sarah asked rather puzzled.

"Look closely at the letters, both names are anagrams of each other."

"Oh, clever clogs!" Louise looked at the card again. "You know, you're right as well!"

Sarah grabbed the card from Louise and stared at it again.

"Why didn't I see that?"

"Probably wood for the trees," Gavin continued.

"Where did you say you got the card from? I can't believe Rebecca gave it to you?" Louise quizzed.

Megan appeared and joined them at their table.

"What's all the excitement?" she asked as she sat down.

"Oh, nothing, we're just discussing your new best friend, Rebecca," Sarah confirmed.

"I'm sure she'll appreciate the attention."

Megan noticed the business card in Sarah's hand and grabbed it from her.

"Thanks, I wondered where that had gone!"

Sarah gave her cousin a thousand dagger stare. "Did you know her names were anagrams? In fact, what do you know about her?"

"No, I didn't, and it's really none of our business," Megan scolded back.

"Ladies, ladies, please! We're on holiday," pleaded Louise.

George had returned to their suite for a second time and was eager to find out from Henry how the events of the afternoon had developed after he had departed. His parents were outside on the balcony. Henry was upstairs. After a quick hello to his parents, George bounded up the stairs.

"Well, Henry, how did it go?"

"Oh, fantastic, thanks. After your kind intervention, our dear parents decided to continue the assault."

George burst out laughing. "Tell me they didn't catch you at it?"

"Thankfully not. Is it your deliberate intention to interfere because I don't need any unwanted surprises like earlier?"

"I was never going to make it easy for you. I'm assuming you have protection in one shape or another?"

Henry looked puzzled.

"Protection?"

"You know, condoms? What stops children becoming an issue."

"Yes, I think I have one somewhere." Henry was on the defensive.

"You don't, do you? And what if the lovely Megan had none either?"

As Henry stood in silence, George wandered across to his suitcase and pulled out a small carrier bag.

"What are you doing?"

George took the bag, opened it and shook the contents on to the bed.

Henry looked on as various condoms fell out onto the bed. There were all shapes, sizes and colours before him, more than he had ever seen before.

"Where on earth did you get these from?" a shocked Henry asked.

"Never mind that. Let's just say a friend of a friend at school."

Henry was now analysing them.

"Wow, I didn't know you could have flavours like these!"

"Oh, we're going to have to go back to basics."

"Our dear parents know nothing of this, of course," Henry stated, quickly thinking of a tactical ploy.

"Our parents aren't going to find out, are they?" George answered too quickly, then smiled at his brother.

"Touché, I think, little brother, and as they don't really know about the sickness the other evening either, I would say a free sample would be a fair exchange for my silence."

George pondered for a few seconds. "I suppose my hands are tied. Apart from anything else, we don't want any little Henrys scurrying around, not at the moment anyway."

"That's quite enough of that, dear brother. What would you recommend, you being an obvious connoisseur?"

"They'll all do the job, if that's what your worrying about."

"I'm assuming you've never actually used any yourself? You know, you being only just sixteen and all that?"

"Of course not, I just provide a service. You never know when some desperate and unfortunate client might have fallen short?"

Henry looked at George with raised eyebrows. "What are you talking about?"

"These are top quality merchandise, Henry. Someone in need will pay handsomely, you know."

"No, I don't think I want to know, thanks."

Henry sheepishly selected his favourite colour and placed it in his drawer.

Back at the bar, Helen and Neil entered and noticed familiar faces before them. They wandered across and sat down.

"We'll have to stop meeting like this," Helen confirmed.

"Hi, Helen, Neil, we were just deciding what we're all doing this evening," Louise replied back.

"Paul and I are taking advantage of the outside and walking round the decks later," Sarah said.

At that moment, a smartly dressed passenger wandered across to the group and looked at Gavin.

"My apologies, I was hoping to speak to the gentlemen who took the IT class this afternoon, was that you, sir?"

"Guilty as charged!"

"Could we have a word in private? I'll buy you a drink at the bar."

Gavin looked rather embarrassed. The rest of the party gave him encouragement.

"OK, but I'm sure I don't owe HMRC anything."

"Oh, it's nothing like that, I promise you."

The two of them moved across to the bar together.

"Come on, Paul, let's go for that walk."

"I don't suppose you fancy another go at blackjack, do you, Helen?" asked Louise.

"Yes, that's fine, is that OK, Neil?" Helen knew full well Neil wouldn't mind.

"That's fine, you go and enjoy yourself, Helen. I'll pop in later and see how you're doing."

"Tell Gavin where I am, will you, please, Megan?" asked Louise.

"Will do."

Sarah had decided they would stroll out along the top decks first where the sun loungers and pools were. The pools had nets over them and it was breezy but sunny. Paul asked her a question.

"Dare I ask, but what are you going to do about Rebecca now?"

"I'm not sure. I'm contemplating."

"If I didn't know you better, I'd say that you were focusing your intentions on Rebecca and forgetting me on this cruise."

"Is that how you feel?"

"At times, yes."

"We'll have to sort that out then. I had been thinking of an early night and all this fresh air might help me get in the mood."

"Now you're talking."

They strolled hand in hand. It was quite quiet and the sound of the sea and open space made for a romantic moment together.

Helen and Louise found two spaces at one side of the blackjack table. Helen ordered a few double shorts for herself. Louise stuck to soft drinks. Having taken another few shorts quite quickly, Helen opened up to Louise again.

"I'm glad I've had you as company while playing this week, Louise."

"Oh, I'm happy to be of help. Anyway, it's just a bit of fun."

"Perhaps this week but it isn't the rest of the time."

"I don't like the sound of that."

Helen ordered another double. "Join me this time, Louise?"

"OK, but a single for me."

"I think I might have a bit of a gambling problem."

Back at the bar, the passenger who had asked for Gavin started his introductions.

"Gavin, my name is Stuart, and I was very impressed with both your classes the last couple of days. Can I ask what you do professionally?"

"I'm an IT manager for our local authority."

"What's your tipple, Gavin?"

"I'll have a malt, thanks, Stuart."

"Good man, I think I'll join you."

The barman soon brought their two malts.

"From your accent, Stuart, I'll guess your West Scotland, Glasgow area?"

"You know your accents. Yes, born and bred. I have an IT consultancy based in Glasgow. We serve mainly small businesses, sole traders, entrepreneurs, that kind of thing. My business partner is retiring in a couple of months and I have been looking for someone to replace him. You were a natural up there, Gavin."

"That's very kind of you to say so, but apart from anything else, I'm based in Inverness and my wife runs a B&B in the area."

"That's OK, I have been looking to service other parts of Scotland outside of Glasgow. I know it's a bit of an 'out of the blue conversation', we're having and, of course, you and your wife would be welcome to pay me a visit in Glasgow and see for yourself our set up."

"Yes, that would be good, Stuart. Are you on your own this week?"

"No, I'm with my wife, but she's gone to see a show. I didn't really fancy it myself. Why don't we have another informal chat, say, tomorrow night? We'll include the wives next time, what do you say?"

"Sounds good. Any decision I make would have to go past the boss, of course?"

"Oh, I completely understand, Gavin."

"I know it's early, but another malt for the road, Gavin, or sea, as is the case here?"

The two of them shared a laugh together.

Suzanne was setting up her equipment for the second time in the sports bar today with her band, the Midnight Jets. They had joined the Atlantic in Lisbon and would leave the ship with the passengers in Southampton. She made a short introduction.

"Good evening, ladies and gentlemen, and welcome to the sports bar again. Thankfully, the storm seemed to have passed us by so I'm not expecting any moving chairs this time."

Some of the passengers laughed in approval.

"We'll be starting in around five minutes."

"Together again, how romantic," Neil said to Megan as they were alone together again at the same table, but across from each other.

"That's not the word I would use."

"Have you seen your boyfriend today?"

"He's not my boyfriend, but yes, I did this afternoon. Do I detect a hint of jealously?"

"Of him! You need a man, not a boy!"

"I'll let you know when I find one!"

Neil shrugged his shoulders and looked to the ceiling. He had noticed Suzanne, who was preparing to start her first song.

"What exactly is 'a bit of a gambling problem'?" Louise asked.

"An online account with several hundreds of pounds in the red."

"Why? When? How?"

"It's a long story."

"I don't think anyone's going anywhere, do you?"

The dealer changed at the tables. There was a break in play.

"Why, because Neil and I work shifts, meaning we're passing like ships in the night. No pun intended either. When, over a period of time, and how, quite easily with all the websites available these days."

"Yes, but gambling surely isn't the answer?"

The dealer was ready and called for bets.

"Do you want to continue playing?" Louise asked.

"Of course, I feel lucky."

"Yeah, and how many times have you said that and not been?"

"Too many to remember, I suppose. It could be worse. I might have succumbed to drink or, even worse, drugs!"

Suzanne was ready to go and introduce their first song. They were due to sing for about forty minutes with a short break in between. For the first half, Megan and Neil sat apart in silence as they listened to the band. Gavin had concluded his conversation and drink with Stuart, and moved across to where Megan was sitting. Simultaneously Neil went to the bar to buy another drink. At the break, Megan went to the ladies and Suzanne moved towards the bar. Neil wasted no time.

"You have a lovely voice."

"Thank you."

"You must build up a thirst. Drink?"

Suzanne hadn't been playing on cruise ships or been away from home for long, but she was glad of any conversation or attention.

"Just a soft one while performing. Orange, thanks."

"Of course. Britvic orange for Suzanne," he asked the waiter. "Have you been with the band long?"

"I need to go back. Are you going anywhere now?"

"I'll stay right here listening."

Suzanne reached her microphone. The bar was filling up.

"So, come on then, Uncle, what did he want?" Megan asked enthusiastically on her return.

"I think I've been offered a partnership in a consultancy."

"You don't sound very sure?"

"I'm not, to be honest, but I'm meeting Stuart and his wife tomorrow, with Louise of course, for another informal chat."

"First impressions?"

"At face value, I'm intrigued, but it's early days. What's with Neil?"

"You're asking me!"

"I'll finish listening to Suzanne, then I'll go and find Louise. You coming with me?"

Megan pondered for a second or two while looking across at Neil. He smiled back, raising his glass.

"Yes, I think I will, Gavin."

Sarah and Paul had come down the decks and were walking once round the ship. Just as they opened the doors to retire inside, someone attracted Sarah's attention.

"That looks like Rebecca?"

"Where? I can't see anyone."

"Come on, let's have a look."

They reached the corridor at the far side and looked both ways. There were other passengers walking along but no sign of Rebecca.

"I could have sworn that was her."

"We're leaving this now?"

"Yes, sorry, Paul. Come on, let's have that early night."

Suzanne and her band finished their set to warm applause. She had soon packed everything away and wandered back across to where Neil was now sitting. Gavin and Megan had left for the casino.

"I've been with the band a couple of years," Suzanne confirmed.

"Sorry?" Neil remarked surprised.

"You were asking me earlier?"

"Yes, I was. You were really very good. Everyone seemed to enjoy the songs. You write them yourself?"

"Most of them, yes."

"Can I get you something stronger?"

"Why not? I have finished playing for today now. Bacardi and Coke, please."

Suzanne was a similar age to Neil and her band, the Midnight Jets, were looking to hit the big time. The opportunity to perform on cruises was ideal to increase their PR and publicity. It did mean a lot of travel away from home and several lonely nights. As the conversation continued, Neil homed in.

Back in the casino, Helen's luck was changing, at least tonight anyway. The new dealer had produced a wave of good hands at the table, resulting in a reasonable gain of around £50. Louise was breaking even and was satisfied. The dealer had changed again.

"That's enough for me tonight. One rule I always follow is to quit while you are ahead, especially when the dealer changes," Louise acknowledged.

"You're not ahead though?" Helen remarked.

"But you certainly are and I'm not letting you lose what you have there."

"I suppose it won't do any harm to win for a change."

"What's the attraction though, Helen, especially online? I can understand to a point the interaction with other players like this."

"I don't know really. There's a buzz about beating the house and it's become almost companionship when I'm home alone."

Just then, Gavin and Megan arrived.

"How did it go with your mystery passenger, Gavin?" Louise enquired.

"Tell you later."

"Where's Neil? I thought he might be with you, Megan?" Helen asked, almost as an afterthought.

"After the band had finished, we left him at the bar," Megan confirmed.

"Oh, I bet I'll be luckier tonight than him."

There was a silence.

"Right, well, busy day tomorrow," Gavin said, trying to move things along.

"Come on Helen, I'm not leaving you here tonight." Louise almost dragged her away from the table.

In the bar, Neil offered Suzanne a nightcap.

"You fancy yourself, don't you?" Suzanne slammed her glass down on the bar.

Neil was taken aback by the remark, which he wasn't expecting.

"I'm tired. I don't specialise in married men, and you're not my type, Neil, so I'll say goodbye."

Suzanne climbed off her chair and was soon talking to another passenger and an officer from CZN.

Neil ordered another drink for himself at the bar. Helen was right. She had been luckier tonight.

17 – FRENCH CONNECTION

Rebecca was up early in the morning and preparing for an excursion that had been arranged at the last moment. Hoping for some company, she knocked on Megan's door. Luckily, Megan had woken earlier and opened the door.

"Morning, what are you doing today?" Rebecca enthused.

"Aw, it's far too early for that level of excitement, but I hadn't anything specific planned."

"How do you fancy accompanying me on an excursion?"

"Where are we going?" There was a pause. "How long do I have?"

"The coach is leaving in just under an hour."

Megan's brain was working overtime.

"Don't I need to book or something?"

"It's all sorted and I'll explain later. Now, are you coming or not?"

"OK, OK, let me phone my aunt and I'll be ready."

Sarah and her family group had a more leisurely breakfast than usual as the ship berthed for the day in La Rochelle. The four of them were going on a boat trip that meandered through the local waterways. Louise updated Sarah and Paul with her cousin's news.

"Megan's already phoned to say Rebecca and her are off on an excursion so it's just us today."

"Surprised, not."

"I think it's good that Megan has found some female company."

Sarah stared menacingly at her uncle.

"That's all I'm saying."

"I'm sure Paul and I saw Rebecca last night at the end of our outside deck walk."

"You thought you did, Sarah. I saw nothing."

"There's still something suspicious about Rebecca."

This time it was Paul who stared at Sarah.

"That's all I'm saying!"

Mary and her husband were looking forward to their trip ashore to explore a traditional castle and town today. Like before, and as a compromise for the boys, Henry and George were coming along, but would be given the remainder of the day and evening to themselves.

"Two days left of our trip and twenty-one tomorrow, big brother! The clock is ticking, in more ways than one."

"Plenty of time left, George. How many times have I told you? We're not all hares like you."

"Just saying, I would hate to win this little bet of ours."

Helen and Neil had launched into rather a drunken argument in their cabin last night, when Neil eventually returned from the bar. They were going on a cognac trip today, which promised to be awkward.

"Are you sure you want to go on this cognac trip? You don't even like cognac," Neil remarked.

"You don't know what I like, which is part of the problem. Anyway, I need to get away from the ship today. I'm going so you can either come with me or not!"

It was a perfect day for the boat trip. The boats gently meandered through the waterways for an hour or so. Time seemed to stand still. Sarah was slouching slightly and had her head on Paul's shoulder. She remembered the canal trip they had shared in Amsterdam on their cruise last year. Gavin and Louise were sitting behind them.

"Aw, look at the two of them. Don't they look good together?" Louise said, turning to Gavin.

"Yes, I suppose so."

"You could sound a little bit more enthusiastic."

"Oh, I am, it's a women thing, all this enthusiasm."

Louise smiled at her husband and settled back in her seat.

Henry and George were a bit bored as they trudged round the castle.

"Remind me why we're here?" George asked.

"It's called a compromise for our parents, which means we have the remainder of the day to ourselves"

You're going to need every second of it to find Megan."

The cognac was going down better than Helen had expected, and after a few, she had temporary forgotten her troubles at home. Neil definitely did not have a taste for it and had decided the silent treatment was better than another argument.

The morning excursions over, the passengers had the remainder of the day to explore La Rochelle or return to *the Atlantic*. Most of them opted for the former.

"Where are we going now?" Megan asked, slightly breathless.

"These two towers make for a perfect viewpoint, don't you think?" Rebecca replied.

"Depends on what we're viewing."

Sarah and family had found an Irish bar and couldn't resist.

"A drink or two, perhaps?" Gavin asked enthusiastically.

"It would be rude not to," Louise replied.

Henry and George were already inside and had sat at the bar.

"I don't want a repeat performance of the other night, George," said Henry

"Oh, don't worry, I want to be sober for the next couple of days."

Neil and Helen had returned from their cognac trip.

"Let's take a walk to those towers," Helen said.

Neil nodded in approval. As they reached the top, they met Rebecca and Megan. Rebecca was taking photographs from the wall.

"What are you photographing?" Neil asked.

"Oh, you get some lovely scenic shots from up here."

"Depends on what you're photographing?" Megan enquired.

"I need to go back to the ship."

"Do you not want to see La Rochelle?"

"No, it's fine. I've seen all I need to today."

Rebecca left the others at the towers. Megan started the conversation.

"Have you been on an excursion today?"

"We've been on a cognac trip," Helen replied.

"Do you like cognac?"

"Neil didn't, but it was OK, I've tasted worse. What are you doing later, Megan?"

There was a moment's silence.

"I'm not sure, I need to find someone."

"I think I might try my luck at blackjack after my win last night."

"You're playing blackjack again?" Neil said, surprised.

"Yes, I like the turn of the cards and trying to beat the house."

"Not really my thing," Megan added.

"There's nothing like the buzz of drawing a blackjack hand."

"Is it not just luck of the cards?"

"You make your own luck, but the skill is looking at the hand you've been dealt and playing the percentages."

"The odds are always against you though, aren't they?"

"Not always. Even when it appears you are up against it, you can pull a rabbit out of the hat," Helen concluded.

Neil interrupted the conversation and pushed the party away from the towers.

"Why don't we have a drink; I saw an Irish pub along the front earlier?"

"I think I'll have a soft one, after all that cognac," Helen said boldly.

"Who did you say you were trying to find?" Neil asked turning to Megan.

"I didn't," Megan responded, with amusement.

The three of them walked along the harbour towards the Irish bar where the others were already sitting comfortably at a table outside. They sat down beside them and waited for a waitress to take their order.

As always, Louise started the conversations.

"Where have you been to today Helen?"

"Cognac trip."

"Do you like cognac?"

"It was OK, I've tasted worse. Neil didn't like it very much. I'm having a soft drink here though."

"Where's your partner in crime, Megan?" Sarah asked with a wry smile.

"Gone back to the ship."

"She was taking some scenic shots from the towers when Helen and I met them both earlier."

There was a break in conversation when drinks were ordered.

"Didn't she want you to go back with her, Megan?" Sarah was pressing again.

"We're not joined at the hip."

"Children, please?" Louise intervened.

Sarah looked to the skies in frustration. Henry and George were looking on from the bar area.

Henry didn't have the courage to just gatecrash the group. George certainly would have, but Henry wasn't having any of it.

"I'm not simply going over there and asking her outright, and neither are you."

"You're going to run out of time and miss an opportunity. Of course, it doesn't bother me, Henry."

"There's tonight and all tomorrow, and given it's my twenty-first, I feel lucky."

"We'll see."

"What's everyone doing tonight?" Louise asked the group.

"Paul and I are having a meal tonight on the upper decks," Sarah enthused.

The whole group sounded, "Woo". Paul went red.

"Aw, I think it's romantic, Paul. Good for you," Louise turned to Paul, giving encouragement. "Gavin and I are speaking to a gentleman about a possible partnership in IT."

We'll see what happens later," Gavin interrupted.

Megan had noticed Henry and George at the bar and was subtly looking their way, while trying to maintain an interest in the group conversation.

"What about you, Megan?" Louise asked.

Megan had drifted across to Henry in her thoughts.

"Looking for someone, apparently," Neil answered for her.

"Megan?" Louise pressed again.

"Sorry, what did you say?"

"Must be love, she's in a daze." Neil concluded, cynically.

Henry and George decided to leave the bar and walk back to the ship. The others stayed for a bit longer. It had been a lovely day in and around La Rochelle, and the party was relaxed as they boarded *the Atlantic* for the penultimate time on board and cruise home to Southampton.

18 – UNDER THE STARS

After yesterday's storm, the weather had turned for the better and was playing ball. *The Atlantic* would have a gentle cruise up the Biscay tonight as it headed towards Guernsey in the morning. Paul and Sarah were readying themselves for dinner.

"I'm just popping out for a minute," confirmed Paul, slightly nervously.

"Where are you going?"

"Won't be long."

With that, Paul was out of the cabin and heading down towards reception.

Gavin, Louise and Megan had dinner together while Sarah and Paul had decided to dine alone elsewhere. Megan was looking a bit lost.

"What are you doing tonight?" Louise quizzed her niece again, after receiving no response in La Rochelle earlier.

"Looking for someone?"

That sounds intriguing," Gavin remarked.

"When are you meeting this couple from last night?" Megan changed the subject.

"After dinner in the coffee bar."

"Oh, it's nice in there. You'll like it."

"You've been to the coffee bar? When was this? I didn't think you liked coffee?" Gavin asked.

"That first morning, when I missed the ship tour. I needed something strong for my head."

Luckily for Paul ,there was no queue at reception and he was back to his cabin in no time.

"Where have you been?" Sarah asked again.

"I was confirming our dinner table." Sarah knew this wasn't true, but played along with it.

"Are we ready?" Paul asked.

"Yes, I'm quite hungry now."

Paul led Sarah up to the restaurant. Although the dress code tonight was smart casual, the pair had made an effort to look their best. After all, it isn't every night you have your evening meal outside on deck under the stars with the view of the sea for company. The restaurant was quiet and there were only a handful of occupied tables, which added to the atmosphere and ambience.

Paul's nerves were beginning to show. Maybe I should have had a malt whisky for Dutch courage, he thought, as the waiter showed them to their seats.

Henry and family were dining in the main restaurant and as promised, the brothers were free to choose tonight's entertainment because their parents were going to watch a show. George was going to the teenagers' club, but Henry was at a loose end.

"Why don't you join us at the show, Henry?" his mother asked.

"Not really my thing, thank you, but you enjoy yourselves. I might hang about the casino and watch the passengers rack up their on board accounts."

"Why don't you both join us for a drink afterwards?"

"Yes, that's fine. When does your show finish?"

"Around half eleven. Shall we say the champagne bar?"

"Yes, that's fine."

"There's a teenage disco on tonight," George intervened.

"Half eleven, George, don't push your luck," Mary confirmed again.

Back on deck under the stars, time was standing still for Paul. They had ordered a starter and a main course and had decided on some wine with their meal. The waiter brought their drinks to the table. The restaurant was quiet, the stars were out and the sun had dropped under the horizon. There was a gentle breeze blowing on deck. The moment was now, he decided. Paul reached for his pocket and simultaneously blurted something out. His heart was pounding.

"Sarah, I have something to ask you?"

"What are you doing, Paul?"

Paul handed Sarah a small blue box.

"What's this?"

"Open it and see."

Sarah opened the box to reveal a shining ring. Some of the tables could be seen from the bar and the waiters had clocked what was going on.

"Sarah, will you marry me and make me very happy?"

After what seemed like a lifetime for Paul, Sarah gave her answer.

"Yes, of course I will!"

Paul stood up and moved round the table towards Sarah. He placed the ring on her finger. They shared a kiss. One or two of the other passengers clapped and cheered. The waiter brought them a bottle of champagne.

"Congratulations, madam, sir. Please accept this bottle on behalf of CZN. Enjoy your evening."

"Thank you," they said together.

The meal was going to be much more relaxed for Paul now.

In the coffee bar downstairs, Gavin and Louise were introduced to Stuart's wife, Rosemary, and the four of them sat down together. The mood was relaxed and friendly.

"I was saying to your husband last night, Louise, how I had enjoyed his IT classes."

"Yes, I think he enjoyed giving them more than he thought he would."

"Have you had a chance to discuss anything since Gavin and I had a chat last night."

"Not really. Gavin's told me the basics but said we would have another discussion tonight."

"That's exactly like Stuart, half a story," his wife intervened.

"Of course, if you were interested, we would have you down in Glasgow for a few days. I was saying to Gavin yesterday, being near Inverness wouldn't necessarily be a problem because we are looking at expanding outside of Glasgow anyway."

"Good, because I have a B&B business in Fort Augustus and we're very happy where we are."

"Oh yes, I said to your husband last night, I completely understood. He quite rightly said it would have to go before the boss first!"

Louise looked at Gavin with approval. Gavin shrugged his shoulders with a smile. The four of them shared a laugh together.

Meanwhile, Helen and Neil made their way down to the casino. Helen sat at the Blackjack table in readiness for the next game. Neil made his way to the gents. Megan noticed Helen at the table and wandered across to her.

"This is where all the action is then?"

"Yes, I guess so. How's Neil?" Helen immediately changed the subject.

"Nothing has happened, if that's what you mean."

"I said to you it wouldn't. When he comes back, take him to the bar, if you would. I get nervous with an audience when I'm playing."

"And do what exactly?"

"Keep him entertained."

Neil came back and stood beside Megan. The dealer was confirming players for the next hand.

"I suggested you both go for a drink. It's not much fun watching me."

Neil turned to Megan and moved to the side to let her through. They walked across to the sports bar together.

Upstairs under the stars, and after the initial excitement in the restaurant on the open deck, the atmosphere had quietened again and passengers were enjoying their evening meals.

"Was it a complete surprise, what just happened?" asked Paul, now enjoying the occasion.

"Yes, but I did wonder when you rushed away from our cabin earlier and I thought you were very nervous just beforehand."

"We should tell your family later tonight."

"Oh no, that can wait until tomorrow! The rest of the night is ours, if you know what I mean?"

"Yes, I think I do."

They finished their drinks including the complimentary bottle of champagne. The night had become very memorable for them both and it was still early evening.

Having left his parents and George behind, Henry sauntered down to the casino to watch the tables in action. The casino was busy but he managed to get a partial view of the blackjack table. As he watched, a female passenger was being dealt several unfortunate hands and had lost a few in a row.

Neil and Megan had ordered their drinks and found a table.

"So, here we are again?" Megan said.

"Yes, we are, and when the cat is away, the mice can play."

"Are you always like this?"

"Only if the person is worth the effort."

"Charming, I'm sure!"

"Are you still chasing your boyfriend?"

"I don't tend to chase anyone. How did it go with Suzanne?"
Suzanne?"

"From the Midnight Jets. That means a no then, if you can't remember from last night! Is all this fruitless chasing not telling you something?"

"That there's plenty of fish in the sea?"

"No, that you're married?"

"I refer you to my previous answer, my lord."

Megan just laughed. Neil looked up behind Megan and saw a young, well-built man staring down at them both. Noticing that Megan was temporary distracted, he smiled back at the young man who walked away.

In the coffee bar, Gavin, Louise, Stuart and Rosemary were having a relaxing evening together. Pleasantries completed, the two wives were having their own conversations, leaving Gavin and Stuart with theirs. As the conversations continued, Louise noticed a young man entering the bar, who she recognised from the other day. He looked a bit despondent. I don't think he's been with Megan, Louise thought, or if he has, it's not gone well.

Megan was enjoying Neil's company at the bar. Whether it was the drinks or the fact that she hadn't seen Henry tonight, there was a lingering almost a 'can't live with/can't live without' scenario going on inside her head.

"You really need to at least see how your wife is doing at blackjack?" Megan asked, but not really caring whether Neil left or not.

"I suppose so, but then what?"

"Maybe your wife might want an early night?"

"I'll go and check, if you promise to buy another round."

Neil walked round to the casino and stood just behind Helen at the table.

"How are you doing?"

"I'm about even, but my luck has turned since earlier."

"Time to quit while you're ahead then?"

"No time, need to keep going and press home the advantage. I'm sure you'll keep Megan amused until I'm finished here."

Neil was slightly taken aback by her comment but didn't argue.

"See you later then?"

"Yes, that's fine."

Helen continued playing. Neil walked back to the bar where another drink was waiting for him.

"That was a strange comment Helen has just come out with," he asked towards Megan.

"Why? What did she say?"

"She was almost requesting me to keep you amused."

Megan chose her next few words very carefully.

"Whatever can she mean by amused?"

"It would seem, not only is the cat away, but it's on extended leave!"

Megan laughed an almost nervous girlish giggle, which set Neil off. What's so funny?"

"Your terminology, extended leave?"

Neil put on a northern accent.

"Come on then love, you've pulled!"

Megan finished her drink, took Neil's hand and led him away from the bar. They walked along the corridor and into the lift. It was empty. They were laughing and giggling while still holding hands. As they walked towards Megan's cabin, they shared a passionate embrace and then again as they reached the door.

"Easy tiger," Megan said trying to find her swipe card.

Neil impersonated a big cat growling. Megan laughed.

"Not, tonight though," she confirmed in a much more serious tone.

Neil ignored the comment and continued his advances.

"No, I'm not joking, Neil."

Neil stood back and stared at Megan. She opened the door, went inside and looked round at Neil, who was still staring back at her.

"And we're stopping now because?"

"You're married and I'm not in the mood. However, tomorrow is our last day on board so anything is possible?"

"I've heard that before!" Neil was now shouting.

"Sshh, you'll disturb the other passengers."

Neil stormed down the corridor back to the casino. Megan closed her door, and although feeling guilty, was very relieved nothing had happened. Had it been Henry, she wouldn't have hesitated. There was always tomorrow though.

Henry had arrived at the champagne bar early and awaited his parents and brother. Having seen Megan with another male passenger, he was feeling totally disheartened. However, it was his twenty-first birthday tomorrow and all was not lost. The rest of his family arrived together. The conversation soon turned to his birthday.

"It's your big day tomorrow, son. What would you like to do?" asked his mother.

"I know what he would like to do!" chirped George.

"I'll pretend I didn't hear that!" their mother scolded back, looking at George.

"Have we booked any excursions yet?"

"No, we haven't, but when your father and I checked earlier today, there were quite a few places available. We would like to go on the vintage coach trip around the island, but you can choose what you wish. Have a look when we're back in our suite."

"One of the guys I met today said there's a cycling tour. What do you say, Henry? You and me against the world?"

"It might do you good for you both to spend some time together away from the ship," their father remarked.

"Yes, some time with my annoying little brother might be just the tonic."

"Right, first thing tomorrow, I'll book it," confirmed Mary.

"Is there a tender tomorrow?" George asked innocently.

"Yes, there is, why?" Mary replied back puzzled.

"It'll be fun watching the elderly negotiate the gap, especially if the sea's rough!"

Henry tried to stop laughing but failed miserably.

"Where did we go wrong with George, John?"

The two brothers were now laughing together. Henry had temporarily forgotten all about Megan.

19 – ISLAND TENDERS

Sarah and Paul were up early. Sarah was not going to waste any time in showing anyone within range her new jewel. First up was her aunt and uncle. She knocked on their door bursting with excitement. Gavin opened the door and stepped back as Sarah bounded in followed closely by Paul.

"Guess what happened last night?" Sarah thrust her hand in the air.

"Paul, what have you gone and done? I did wonder what you had left at reception that day we boarded," Gavin said immediately.

"You're not happy?" Sarah asked, looking perplexed.

"Of course, I am delighted for you both," Gavin confirmed.

Louise screeched and grabbed Sarah's hand to have a look at the ring.

"We'll need to celebrate this afternoon. Everyone round here for a family party!"

Gavin and Paul looked on and shook hands.

"I think this is where I say welcome to the family, Paul."

"Thank you, Gavin. I'm glad it's done. I was very nervous last night."

"Engaged on a cruise, how romantic!" Louise was still screeching.

Gavin and Paul looked at each other and sighed.

"Does Megan know?" Louise had come back down to earth.

"No, she doesn't, but she soon will," Sarah said with a wry smile.

In their family suite on the upper deck, Henry was up early. He was twenty-one today and was going to enjoy some family time. He walked down the stairs to find his parents already up.

"Happy birthday, son," they said in stereo.

There were several '21st' birthday balloons tied to the chairs at the table and a present on it.

Henry walked across to the table and started opening the small box. It was a gold, Swiss watch.

"Thank you, it's wonderful! You shouldn't have."

"Yes, we should have. There's no excuse for being late for work now," his father joked towards Henry.

Henry smiled, kissed his mother on the cheek and shook his father's hand.

"After the excursions this morning, we should order room service for lunch and champagne to celebrate," confirmed his mother.

"I'll enjoy that, thanks." Henry ran back up the stairs. George was now awake.

"Happy birthday, big brother!" George took something from his drawer and passed it to Henry. It was in the shape of a book.

As Henry started unwrapping the paper, the book revealed all. His face went red.

"*Sex: Dating: The Gentleman's Guide to Effortless Seduction.*"

"No excuses now."

"I don't know what to say, George, and I'm not even going to ask how, why or where."

George reached for another present and passed it to Henry.

"Happy birthday, Henry, seriously this time."

Henry opened it to reveal an exclusive pen set.

"Thank you, George, very practical for once!"

"Seeing that you're working for the family now."

"When our parents ask what you got me for my birthday, I think I'll mention the latter and hide the former."

"Probably best."

The brothers shared a laugh together.

The Atlantic had berthed outside the harbour and the ship's tenders would be used to ferry the passengers ashore. The sea was unusually calm today and because CZN had operated this several times before, it was run like a military operation. Today's stop was only for half a day or so. Gavin, Louise, Helen and Neil were on a walking trip to the local castle; Sarah, Paul, Megan and Rebecca were on a rigid inflatable boat; Mary and John were riding on a vintage coach, and Henry and George were on an organised bike trip.

Sarah and Paul met up with the other passengers at the quayside before their speedboat trip. Megan and Rebecca were close by.

"Paul and I got engaged last night under the stars. It was so romantic!" Sarah thrust her left hand towards them.

"Congratulations for you both," Rebecca announced.

"Paul, I told you to let her down gently at the end of the cruise," Megan said, rather sarcastically.

There was a slight pause.

I'm very happy for you both," Megan continued. "When's the wedding?"

"Calm down, ladies, we're only just engaged," Paul replied.

"You'll be the first to know, cousin, don't worry."

After the initial safety instructions from their guide, Henry and George were off cycling in their group of around a dozen.

"Last day for our 'challenge', Henry. You're running out of time."

"Yes, but what a day it would be on my twenty-first and all!"

"You don't know where her cabin is, so how are you going to meet her?"

"All in good time."

"Tick tock, tick tock!"

The group stopped at a country store for a break. Henry and George were last to arrive and sat at the edge of the party. Henry went inside the store with most of the other passengers. When he returned, there were two other large teenagers beside George and a skirmish was developing.

"Give me your bike, son, there's a good boy."

"You're joking!" George shouted, when he was pushed to the ground by the other boy.

Henry rushed across and stood behind the two threatening teenagers.

"What do we have here?"

The two boys turned round quickly and Henry stood right in front of them both. He was taller than them and with an obviously strong and fit physique, which would easily have overcome them both.

"Go and pick on someone your own size," he said, boldly.

The two backed off rapidly.

"You OK, George?"

"I am now, thanks."

Henry took one aggressive pace forward and the two intruders started running in the opposite direction.

George had seen a different side of his brother for the first time today. The guide and CZN crew member walked across to investigate the commotion.

"Is everything alright? What did they want?"

"Oh, just a couple of bullies, we're OK," Henry confirmed. His heart was pounding. Henry helped his brother up.

"OK, everyone, let's continue our ride. Please stay together as much as possible," the guide confirmed.

"You ready to continue, George?"

"You bet, big brother, you bet!"

Megan and Rebecca had become separated from Sarah and Paul.

"I think Sarah and Paul make a lovely couple, don't you, Megan?"

"Yes, they do. Under the stars though?"

"I can think of worse places?"

"At least this distraction might get Sarah off your back now."

"I didn't think she was?"

"Oh, once she gets her teeth into something, she's like a dog with a bone!"

Her cousin's engagement had served as a reminder to Megan that a long-term commitment was a low priority, but conversely something more casual was definitely worth pursuing.

20 – FAMILY FUN

With all the passengers having safely negotiated the tenders and back on board, *the Atlantic* headed slowly towards Southampton. This evening's sailing was promising to be short, calm and quiet.

Henry's mother, as promised, had ordered a room service banquet for the four of them. The family had a double birthday to celebrate after all; Henry's twenty-first today and John's sixtieth next week. It took two crew members with a large trolley to bring their evening feast to their suite.

"I don't think I've seen as much food ever before," George remarked.

"I won't need to eat on this ship again after this," Henry added.

Their mother, Mary, was organising everything.

"Come on, boys, don't just look at it, help yourselves."

There was plenty of champagne on offer as well. The suite had an extended balcony, which easily accommodated the four of them. They sat together watching the sea.

"This takes us back, John, to those early days when we took the yacht out and the boys were much younger."

"Yes, it seems a long time ago now, though?"

"It does, but we were happy and life was simpler back then."

The boys were playing violins with their hands, mocking slightly.

"Youngsters today, they know nothing," John reiterated.

"Completely different generation, John, it's not their fault."

Meanwhile, Sarah and party had decided to try the pizza restaurant for an early evening snack before heading towards the champagne bar for a celebration drink.

"Any thoughts on the wedding, Sarah?" Louise enthused.

"Louise, they've only just got engaged!" Louise gave Gavin that look.

"Already asked, Aunt," Megan chipped in.

"As it came as a bit of a surprise, no, we haven't yet, thanks."

"How was your excursion on the speedboat?" Louise asked instead.

"Different. Rebecca and I enjoyed it, thanks."

"You've enjoyed her company this week, Megan?" Gavin hesitantly asked.

Sarah intervened first. "There's still something..."

Paul interrupted. "Which is not our concern."

"Well said Paul!" Megan smiled back at Sarah.

"Children!" Louise scowled at Gavin.

"It was an innocent question!"

Megan changed the subject.

"And your excursion?"

"Yes, a relaxing walk round the castle."

"Spoiled somewhat by our cabin neighbours arguing," Gavin looked round expecting a response from Louise.

"They are obviously having some marital problems."

"I refer to my previous answer, me lord," Paul said with a hint of conclusive sarcasm.

Back in the family suite, Henry and George caught a few minutes alone together.

"I've never seen you act like you did earlier before, Henry, when you rescued me from those bullies ashore, but I liked what I saw, thank you."

"I'll take that as a compliment. And while we're in a good mood, one good turn deserves another, I think?"

"Let me guess, Megan?"

"Although I hate to admit it, I am running out of time."

"Just leave it to George, I'll come up with a plan."

Their mother, always alert, had overheard.

"What plan is this, boys?"

"Oh, just another part of Henry's twenty-first."

"I don't want you getting into any mischief!"

"As if we would, Mother?"

"Yes, given half the chance! Your father and I are going to the theatre again tonight. I trust you'll stick together and keep yourselves amused, responsibly?"

"That's my middle name!" George laughed!

The family party of five finished their light meal and walked round to the champagne bar. It was busy but there was one table left. They sat down and were soon approached by a waiter who took their order. They all decided on celebratory champagne, of course. Megan recognised the seating immediately as she had sat here with Henry only two days earlier.

The waiter brought their drinks across.

"Cheers, and congratulations to you both!" Louise proclaimed.

There was much tingling of glasses.

"Are you coming with us to the theatre tonight, Megan?" Louise asked.

"I think I'll pass, thanks. I'm looking for someone."

"Not Rebecca, for once!" Sarah gave a wry smile towards Megan.

"She's all yours, if you wish, Sarah."

"One thing we do all have to do tonight is pack," Louise continued.

"Yes, but not until later, let's enjoy the moment. There is more champagne back at our cabin," Gavin confirmed.

The remaining glasses were downed and they all left for Louise and Gavin's cabin, for one final drink together.

Back in the family suite and having consumed more food than ever before, Henry and George were sitting on the balcony watching the sea together. Their parents had gone inside the suite.

"You were talking about a plan earlier, George?"

"All in good time, Henry, all in good time."

Time was suddenly something Henry was running out of.

21 – FULL HOUSE

As part of the on board entertainment at sea, CZN had bingo in the afternoons, and Sandra would be hosting this activity in the show lounge. The jackpot stood at £1,000, which would easily clear most passengers' outstanding accounts.

Helen and Neil had decided to try their luck. They entered the lift on one of the top decks. The lift was empty as they made their way down and was stopping at each floor as more passengers entered. Several of them were obvious bingo pros with their own pens and pencils. By the time the lift had descended to its destination, there were about a dozen passengers inside and you could have cut the atmosphere with a knife. As they exited the lift, another couple of lifts also arrived which were crammed full of bingo hungry passengers. The lounge area was filling up fast when Helen and Neil entered. They grabbed one of the few remaining seats and settled down, having collected their cards for the games. The anticipation in the lounge area was building with much small talk. Sandra had just finished checking the electronic machine with one of the engineers.

"Good afternoon, ladies and gentlemen. Our first bingo game is due to start shortly. Please make sure you have your playing cards ready. I will confirm which ones you need to be using before each game."

Rebecca had decided to attend the bingo as well this afternoon. She had arrived early and was one of the first passengers there, which meant she had a good spot in the lounge area.

"We could do with a bit of luck this afternoon," Helen said turning to Neil.

"Maybe this could be a turning point."

Sandra was about to start.

"Ladies and gentlemen, if everyone is ready, we'll start the first game. We are playing with the green coloured game cards."

The first couple of games passed quite quickly. There were five games in total, including the jackpot at the end with the £1,000 prize. The penultimate game required two complete lines and gave £250 to the winner. You could have heard a pin drop in the room until...

House!" Helen erupted in excitement, as her last number required was called.

"Well done, madam, we just need to check your numbers," Sandra said.

Numbers were checked and confirmed.

"Congratulations, you've won £250!"

"See, I told you this could be our turning point," Neil said.

At the same time, Henry and George were continuing their conversation on the balcony of their family suite.

We don't know where Megan's cabin is, do we?" George asked.

"No, I don't, nor her surname nor where the rest of her family's cabins are."

"She's been here, of course."

"Yes, but that's not much help."

Back in the show lounge, Sandra started the final game. There was great anticipation in the room. As each number was called out, several passengers were one number nearer winning.

"Is anyone near yet?" Sandra checked progress.

There were several groans from the passengers. After a few more numbers, there was a rather muted shout from across the floor.

"House."

All eyes turned to the passengers as a winning claim had been made. There was a resignation among the remaining passengers.

That's interesting, thought Rebecca, as she looked over her shoulder, it's the same couple who won the 80s quiz.

"Let's check those numbers," said Sandra to her colleague.

There were mutterings from several of the other passengers. Apparently the couple who had won hadn't attended the bingo earlier in the week. The winning numbers were confirmed. Just as during the 80s quiz, the winning couple looked rather sheepish when they collected their winnings. The lounge quickly emptied out as most passengers left, leaving one or two to stay with their drinks and thoughts of what could have been. Rebecca returned to her cabin.

"This win means a final play of the blackjack tonight," Helen said.

"Why don't we keep it, for when we get back, or we could use it to partially pay our account?" Neil offered some suggestions.

"We'll see. This could be our lucky night."

They left together and headed back to their cabin.

While the bingo was wrapping up the two brothers continued their conversation.

"It isn't, unless Megan came here, of course?" George said.

"Apart from making a tannoy announcement, I don't know how that's going to happen."

"I'll stay here for a while in case she does. You have a walk round and try and find her."

"Needle in a haystack comes to mind."

"Where's all this negativity suddenly coming from? You handled those bullies earlier on today, so this should be a piece of cake!"

"Yes, of course, there are only around 3,500 passengers on board. I bet she's the first one I see tonight?" There was obvious sarcasm in Henry's voice.

"What was it my namesake used to say? I love it when a plan comes together!"

"You're far too young to remember that, and anyway, it's slightly different here?"

"Have faith Henry, have faith."

22 – FIRST TIME FOR EVERYTHING

Sarah and her family group had made their way to the theatre for the final production of the cruise. Megan was left in the sports bar contemplating what to do next.

Helen, spurred on from her earlier bingo win, was having one more shot at blackjack. Neil left her at the tables and wandered across to the sports bar. He soon spotted Megan and walked to her table, sitting down beside her.

"If we continue to meet like this, people will think we're having an affair," Megan said.

"Which, of course, we're not. Not yet anyway."

Megan laughed. "There isn't going to be an affair."

"I realise that now."

"Does this mean you're going to give your marriage another chance?"

"I guess it does. One last drink for the road?" Neil asked in a soft tone.

"Why not? It couldn't hurt."

As Neil was about to go to the bar, a waiter stopped him and took his order.

At the same time, Henry and George were alone in their suite having seen their parents leave for the theatre.

"It is time, big brother."

"I don't know where to start."

"Like I said, the casino and sports bar is your starter for ten. I'll stay here for a bit. Give it about fifteen minutes and come back."

Henry left their suite and walked along the corridor. This was completely outside his comfort zone and his heart was pounding violently inside his chest. To try and steady himself, he wandered up to Nevis's bar and ordered a double vodka. As soon as it arrived, it was downed in one. Dutch courage, he thought, as he left Nevis's and made his way down to the casino.

"What are you going to do for the rest of the evening?" Neil asked.

"I need to find someone."

"Ah, the young boyfriend."

"Perhaps."

Helen's luck was running out, and after a bad session in the casino, a change of dealer called for a change of scene. She walked into the bar just in time to see Megan and her husband together.

Henry bypassed the casino and headed straight for the sports bar as his brother had suggested. He followed a group of passengers in, but his view was partially blocked.

"I need to check on how Helen is doing."

"That's the best thing I've heard you say all week."

"I'll walk with you to the entrance."

They got up from their seats. Megan gave Neil a big kiss on the cheeks. As they moved away, Neil temporarily put his arm round Megan and gently nudged her forward. They shared a smile and laugh together, oblivious as to who was looking on.

Rebecca was having a quiet night, at least initially, in her cabin. She had a meeting with Craig later on and had some things to prepare.

Megan left Neil and walked briskly towards one of the two suites she had spent some time in the other day with Henry. Within a minute or two, she was knocking on the door. George, thinking it was his brother, was talking as he opened the door.

"You're a bit previous, aren't you?" He said, without looking as he spoke.

George and Megan were now facing each other.

"Who is?"

"Sorry?"

"Who's previous?"

"Henry, and he has clearly not found you."

"He was looking for me?"

"Bloody hell, it's like I'm talking to him now. Yes, of course he is."

"Can I come in?"

"Sure." George stood to the side as Megan entered.

Henry's heart sank as he made his way back to his suite. However, when he opened the door with his swipe card, there was a surprise waiting for him inside.

Back in the sports bar, Helen wasn't thinking straight. I should never have asked her in the first place. I mean I never thought he would actually go through with it. There was one place she wanted to go, but beforehand, she needed to call in a favour from the Cabin Steward.

Meanwhile in the family suite, "Megan?" Henry blurted out.

"Guilty as charged."

"But I've just seen you with someone else."

"Oh, at the bar, yes. His cabin was between my cousin and my aunt and uncle's so I've been in his company a few times, that's all."

"Time to seize the moment," George said to his brother.

"Would you like a drink?" Henry asked.

"I think I've had enough already."

"Can't stay here, might get interrupted again."

"We'll have to do something about that then."

"Have you got your favourite colour, Henry?"

George swung his head upstairs. Henry's face went a bright red.

"Is this some brotherly code?"

Henry was already running upstairs.

"You'll find out later," George said, looking at Megan.

Henry came back down the stairs. Megan took his hand and opened the suite door.

"Enjoy yourselves. Go easy on my big brother, Megan, he's a bit shy."

Megan smiled as the door closed. They walked hand in hand towards her cabin, laughing and joking together, and obviously pleased to have found each other.

Helen was playing a waiting game. As she stood in total darkness, a million thoughts were going round in her head and the future at this point wasn't looking encouraging. She could hear approaching laughter, which got louder until it was almost beside her.

Megan stopped outside her cabin and turned to Henry. They shared a passionate embrace against the door, before she finally opened it. Megan was giggling and Henry laughing. Megan turned the main light on within the cabin while Henry walked to the bathroom. Now half-naked, he turned the light on just as a female figure stumbled out from the shower. Helen gathered herself together to reveal a young, half-naked man looking at her in amusement. He smiled at her. Megan realised there was something wrong.

"What's the matter, Henry?" She said, slightly alarmed.

Helen decided that attack was the best form of defence.

"You're not my husband?" She managed to say, curtly.

Henry stood in silence as Megan moved beside him revealing herself to Helen.

"What are you doing in my shower?" Megan said to Helen.

Helen wasn't backing down.

You were with my husband earlier," she accused Megan.

"Yes, I was saying goodbye to him, but clearly I am not now!"

"I'll leave you ladies to it then," Henry said very softly, backing away slightly.

Megan blocked Henry's retreat.

"You're going nowhere. Helen is leaving!" Megan said, taking charge. Megan was casting a thousand daggers towards Helen.

"It seems I didn't know my husband at all. You kids enjoy yourself and don't do anything I wouldn't," Helen said to them both, to save her obvious embarrassment! Helen moved sheepishly out of the bathroom and towards the door.

"Go back to your husband, Helen," Megan said generously.

Helen opened the door and when it had closed, she pressed her back hard against it, breathing fast. Although extremely embarrassed, the end result could have been a thousand times worse. She walked away from Megan's cabin and back towards the casino.

"Now, where were we?" Megan said seductively.

"Being interrupted again," Henry replied.

"We'll have to do something about that then."

Megan opened her cabin door as Helen reached the end of the corridor, turning out of sight. She placed the 'Please do not disturb' card on the door handle and closed it behind her.

"Now where were we?" she said again to Henry.

Helen smiled to herself. She was certain the couple within the cabin wouldn't reveal the last few minutes to anyone else and she certainly had no intention of doing so either.

23 – REBECCA'S REVELATION

Sarah and party had enjoyed the show and made their way towards the entrance and down the corridor to where several of the performers were standing. The line of passengers was at a standstill and forming an orderly queue as pleasantries were exchanged. Sarah looked ahead to see Rebecca in the distance. She turned round and smiled at her before disappearing from view.

"That was Rebecca up there," Sarah said.

"I didn't see her, Sarah and I'm not goose-chasing," Paul responded.

"Come on, we won't be long."

Paul looked round to Louise and Gavin as he was dragged away by Sarah. He frowned and looked to the heavens!

"Good luck with that one, Paul," Gavin shouted as he watched them dart between the passengers ahead of them, hand in hand.

"Can we have one final drink before we have to finish packing?" Louise asked despondently.

"Yes, why not?"

Sarah and Paul reached the corner where she had seen Rebecca.

"If Rebecca was here, she's gone now," Paul said.

Sarah started looking around.

"Of course," she said pointing to a door that read, 'Staff only'.

"No way, and look, there's a code needed, which we don't know. Actually, what do I mean, we're not going there!"

They both stood against the wall beside the door. Without warning, the door opened. It was their Cabin Steward.

"Oh, Austin, it's you! What fantastic timing!" Sarah couldn't believe her luck.

"Good evening, madam, sir. Is everything OK?"

"Yes, thank you, but we just need to see Craig, the Cruise Director." Sarah was thinking fast as she went along.

There was a moment's pause. Austin was hesitating.

"I'm not sure, madam, if it's allowed for passengers to enter this area."

"No, it's fine, really. My uncle volunteered to take the two IT classes earlier this week, so we need to speak to Craig about it."

"OK madam, sir, but you won't tell anyone, will you?"

"Your secret's safe with us, Austin."

Austin gingerly opened the door and started to walk down a flight of stairs.

"What on earth are you going to say if we're stopped, or seen for that matter?" Paul asked as they followed him down.

"I'll worry about that when it happens."

"Why did you ask for Craig?"

"I saw him with Rebecca, and I'm sure he's involved anyway, so I can use Gavin's IT class again if we're stopped. Come on, we're going to lose Austin."

Sarah and Paul were lead down the stairs to a long corridor where several crew members were walking along. Coming the other way was Austin's manager, who stopped to ask what was going on.

"Hello, Austin, what are you doing?"

"These two passengers want to see Craig."

"The Cruise Director doesn't meet passengers down here in his office. You know that, Austin."

"It's our fault, we asked, no, we persuaded Austin to bring us down here. I really wanted to see Craig," pleaded Sarah.

"It's true, she's been driving me insane all week," Paul said.

Austin's manager gave out the faintest of smiles.

"Very well madam, sir, follow me, please. That's fine, Austin, I'll take it from here."

Austin scampered back towards the stairs.

"I don't want Austin blamed for this, it really isn't his fault," Sarah remarked, boldly.

"Certainly, madam, follow me."

Sarah and Paul were lead further along the corridor until they reached several staff offices.

"Wait here, please," instructed the Cabin Manager.

"We're for it now," Paul said.

Meanwhile back upstairs, when Helen returned to the casino, Neil was waiting for her.

"Where have you been? I've looked everywhere for you," he said with relief, as she appeared.

"I needed to go back to the cabin for something," she lied to him.

"Why didn't you tell me about your gambling?"

"I don't know what you mean."

"I've seen your account statement. You've lost hundreds of pounds recently."

"I didn't think you cared."

"I'm your husband, it's my job to care."

"You have a funny way of showing it."

"Let's just say this week has been a bit of an eye opener for me. When we get home, why don't we see if one or both of us can change our work shifts. It's not helping that we hardly see each other, and we're living like ships passing in the night."

"You're serious about that, Neil? You'd change your shifts for me?"

"If it meant spending more time together, then yes. In return, you'll cancel your online account?"

"Deal", Helen said, now smiling at her husband at last.

Two seats together were free at the blackjack table.

"Fancy a game of blackjack?" Helen asked.

"I don't really know how to play."

"Just as well you have an excellent teacher then."

They laughed together as they took their seats, holding hands for the first time in a while.

Back down in the staff quarters, Sarah and Paul had been standing for a while, when the Cabin Manager suddenly returned.

"Craig will see you now. Follow me, please."

Sarah whispered to Paul as they followed. "Told you we'd be alright."

Paul shrugged his shoulders. They entered an office where Craig was sitting at one desk and Rebecca at the other.

"Sarah, Paul, how can I help you?" Craig said the moment they stepped inside the compact office.

There was a moment's pause. Rebecca was smiling in the corner. Sarah was on autopilot as she launched right in on the offensive.

"You know Rebecca well?" she asked Craig.

"Yes, why?" he replied.

"She's been acting very strangely this week and I knew her sister whom I didn't take to. I know it's none of my business, but you're not having an affair, are you?" Sarah continued.

Craig and Rebecca looked at each other and laughed.

"No, we're not having an affair," Rebecca said.

"I didn't think it was that funny!" Sarah shouted.

"You didn't like mine and Megan's friendship, did you?"

"Megan has a tendency to lead my younger sister, Hannah, astray and she took it too far last year at my parent's funeral."

"Clearly some history there," Rebecca said.

Craig changed the subject.

"I see congratulations are in order for you both."

"Yes, thank you, Craig," said Paul.

"I believe you proposed at dinner on the outer decks."

Paul looked slightly bewildered. "Yes, but how do you know?"

"There's not much happens on this ship that I don't hear about." Craig continued. "Having become engaged on board *the Atlantic* with us at CZN, I hope you'll consider spending your honeymoon with us as well."

Craig reached for one of his business cards and handed it to Sarah." Drop me an email and I'll make sure we make it worth your while. I'm sure we can throw in several special offers for you both." Sarah accepted the card, almost grudgingly.

"That's very kind, thank you," Paul said.

"Which leaves the question about Scarlet Pimpernel in the corner!" Sarah was really pushing her luck now.

Craig chuckled to himself. Rebecca gave Sarah a killer glance.

"We're only having this conversation because your uncle did a great job with his IT classes and really dug us out of a hole. Over to you, Scarlet Pimpernel."

"To cut a very long story short, I'm a PI," Rebecca said, at last.

There was a long pause.

"Wow, like Magnum!" Paul blurted out.

"Sort of, but without the Ferrari!"

"I liked the anagram names, by the way," Paul said.

"Thank you, I thought it added a little intrigue," Rebecca replied.

"Who have you been following?" Paul asked.

"You remember the couple who won the quiz at the 80s night?"

"Yes, they did collect their award rather sheepishly now you come to mention it," Paul said.

"Earlier today, they also won the jackpot at bingo. Unfortunately, for them, their luck is about to run out. It turns out they aren't a couple at all, in a manner of speaking. They are having an affair and one of them is known to our family and the other person's other half is known to Craig!"

"You're suddenly quiet, Sarah," Craig remarked.

"You're a Private Investigator? That explains the strange behaviour at least!" She said slowly, in response to Craig's question

"Does this appease you now?" Rebecca asked Sarah.

"I suppose so, but it leads to more questions than answers."

"Which we're not going to ask or investigate any more, are we, Sarah?" Paul intervened. "Thank you both, I think we can safely leave it there?" Paul turned to Sarah, now taking charge of the situation.

Sarah nodded reluctantly when Paul turned to the door, making his exit. They left the room and Paul thanked them both again.

"There's more to it than that, right?" Sarah was pleading to find out more.

"I don't think so and it's none of our business, anyway," Paul confirmed as they made their way back along the corridor to the stairs.

Craig and Rebecca looked at each other back in the office, behind the closed door.

"Sarah is a smart one. She knows there was more than what we were telling her," Craig said.

"Thankfully Paul was there to hold her back, otherwise it could have been a bit awkward," Rebecca replied.

"Particularly the part about our affair, a few years back, you mean?"

They smiled at each other.

"I keep a bottle of wine here in my cupboard. One for old times sake?" asked Craig.

"Why not."

Craig poured the wine and they toasted each other's good health.

24 – THAT WAS THE CRUISE THAT WAS

Louise and Gavin sat in the sports bar for the last time reflecting on the past week.

"Have you enjoyed your first cruise?" Gavin asked.

"Definitely, and I'm certain it won't be our last. You do remember I'm still owed a bottle of champagne?"

"Oh yes, I almost forgot about that. We'll buy something when we're back home."

"Make sure you do," Louise confirmed.

"Most memorable moment of the cruise?" Gavin continued.

"Our niece getting engaged, that came out of nowhere. What about you, though? IT extraordinaire!"

"I surprised myself with that one, I must admit."

"A possible new career as well?"

Gavin shrugged his shoulders.

"There's a lot of dotting Is and stroking Ts yet, though, if it goes that way."

"I really hope Helen and Neil can sort themselves out," Louise said.

"They can certainly argue, that's for sure."

"Then there's our Megan!"

"You say that as if she did something wrong?"

"Well, chasing two guys at the same time and one of them married!"

"No harm done?"

"Not really the point though! Men, you don't realise the consequences!"

"You're a bit of a social butterfly, aren't you, dear?"

"I'm a woman, it's my job to know what's going on. I run a B&B, remember? You wouldn't believe the stories I hear at breakfast!"

Gavin nearly spilled his drink.

"A bit early in the morning for all that?"

"Don't you believe it!

"They go into graphic details?"

"Sometimes. Guests are on their holidays, they're much more relaxed."

"I'm in the wrong profession!" Gavin continued. "Talking of Megan, I wonder if she ever found out what Rebecca was up to?"

I don't know, but it was certainly annoying Sarah."

"She was good company for Megan, I suppose. I did like her anagram names, quite clever really."

Back in Megan's cabin, Henry looked at his watch. It was a quarter to twelve. Still fifteen minutes left of my birthday, he thought. I must have dozed off. He rose out of the bed quietly and looked behind him. Megan was lying there asleep. That was the best twenty-first birthday present. He smiled as he dressed and tiptoed to his shoes. Deciding not to put them on, he continued to the cabin door. He opened the door as quietly as he could and looked round a final time. As he closed the door, Megan stirred. However, she was happy and tired and she simply went straight back to sleep, smiling contently to herself.

Henry left the cabin a different person to the one who had entered it earlier. There is a first time for everyone and as he walked along the corridor, still holding his shoes, he reflected on his own future and the family business. It can be quite eerie walking along a seemingly empty ship at night, he thought.

He was soon at his family suite. He opened the door and turned round, still trying to be quiet.

It didn't matter because his mother was there making coffee, as if she knew what her eldest son was up to.

"Join me for a coffee, son?" her mother asked in a comforting tone.

"Why not?"

"Have you enjoyed yourself this week, Henry?"

"Yes, it's been interesting."

Mary poured them both a coffee.

"That time the other day, during the storm, when we came back from the IT class, were you entertaining that young girl whose uncle was taking the class?" Mary got straight to the point with her son.

"No!" What makes you ask that?"

"Henry, I'm your mother, I know you inside out."

"Even if I was, father would never have approved of such a thing."

"Your father loves you and your brother dearly, he simply struggles sometimes to show it. You'd be surprised at what he will tolerate. Anyway, you leave him to me."

Henry raised a smile, feeling tired, himself now.

"We had a bit of a father son talk the other day as we drew into Lisbon."

"Yes, he did mention something earlier. He's very proud of you taking a part in the family business, Henry."

"I feel sometimes that George gets away with murder compared to what I had to endure."

"Your upbringing wasn't that strict, was it?"

"No, I suppose not."

"Pitfalls of being the eldest, Henry."

Henry had finished his coffee. They rose together. Henry kissed his mother on the cheek.

"What was that for?"

"For being an excellent mother and listening."

"That's my job, son."

Henry ran quietly upstairs to his room. George was half-asleep but Henry was bursting to tell him the events of earlier. Of course, George knew what had happened before Henry spoke!

"You've only gone and done it, haven't you?!"

Henry gave a very broad smile.

"My job here is done!" George exclaimed. The brothers exchanged a high-five.

Meanwhile, Louise and Gavin were still reminiscing about the success of their first cruise.

"It's a real shame we are leaving this beautiful ship tomorrow," Louise groaned.

"Which will make our next cruise worth looking forward to."

"I quite fancy the Caribbean. We could go in the New Year when the B&B is closed, and by then you'll be your own boss!"

"We'll see."

"Imagine all the places we can visit, which we couldn't possibly travel to independently?"

"You've caught the cruise bug then."

"Hasn't the last week been fabulous though? Six-star service; being treated like royalty; exquisite dining; and I don't think I've ever sampled so much champagne. I'm so relaxed and actually feel like I've had a holiday. This is lifestyle changing. The future's bright, Gavin, and it's on a cruise!"

"You should get a job in the cruise industry, you've sold it to me anyway!"

At that moment, Sarah and Paul came into view and headed towards them.

"You are not going to believe what we've found out about Rebecca! I'll tell you in a minute, but I've got a question to ask, especially for you, Gavin." Sarah said immediately.

"OK," Gavin answered, hesitantly.

"In the absence of my father, would you give me away at my wedding, please?" Sarah asked, politely.

There was a short pause.

"I don't know what to say, Sarah," Gavin replied with a hint of emotion. "I'd be delighted and honoured, thank you!"

They shared a silent hug.

"That's the first box ticked for the wedding," Sarah said.

"Looking forward to it already!" Louise added.

The Atlantic cruised effortlessly towards Southampton. When she docked in the morning, all the passengers would leave and make their journeys back home taking with them the memories of their cruise.

NAUTICAL NIGHTS

It has only been since writing the first two books in the Sailaway Trilogy I have started blogging.

The original title was going to be *Ninety-Nine Nautical Nights* or *Nine Nautical Nights*. However, I dropped the numbers when I decided to write them as a series of themed cruises, each with six parts. *Nautical Nights* took shape and I published online in November 2016, with the first cruise, *Tour de France*. The first six parts are printed here, but you can find many more adventures for the Captain, crew and passengers of CZN's two sister ships online on my website at http://www.sailaway.voyage/nautical-nights and https://niume.com/profile/97994#!/posts

I thoroughly enjoyed writing *Nautical Nights* and I hope you have fun reading them too! You can follow these adventures each calendar month, every Tuesday. Bon voyage and happy sailing!

Derek Curzon

http://www.sailaway.voyage/nautical-nights
https://niume.com/profile/97994#!/posts

Cruise 1; Part 1: The Captain's in deep water, even in the shallows.

"We now go over to our roaming reporter 'Rendez Vous', who is quayside with the Captain, preparing for his latest voyage."

"As you look back, Captain at your career, do you have any regrets?"

"None at all, my dear."

"Not even that corruption scandal which ultimately stopped you becoming Commander?"

There was a brief pause.

"That was a long, long time ago. Unusual name you have, Mrs Vous. French. I presume?"

"Please, Captain, call me Rendez and yes, it is. On the subject of names, this brand new ship, *SS Sunset*, It sounds like a cruise for those on their way out!"

"I sincerely hope not. Her sister ship is the *SS Sunrise* so we've hopefully struck a happy balance."

Suddenly a man came rushing along on a bicycle wearing a polka dot shirt and waving a bag of onions around his head.

"Vive La France!" he shouted, or something similar.

Rendez jumped out of the way. Captain Kibosh wasn't so lucky and by stepping backwards to avoid the onions....

SPLASH!!!

The poor Captain hit the water like a stone. He was clearly struggling.

"Swim to me, Captain!" shouted Rendez.

The Captain tried to respond but was drowned out by the swell. By now there was a small crowd at the water's edge.

"He can't swim!" confirmed the First Officer who had seen the commotion.

"The Captain can't swim?" Rendez asked, looking perplexed.

"Oh my god, are you OK, Captain?" said Miss Fortune, ZNC's PR Executive.

"He's never liked the water," the First Officer continued.

Miss Fortune threw the Captain a lifebuoy.

Part 2: Bagpiper Jock & the First Officer are misunderstood.

ZNC had pulled out all the stops for the launch of their brand new ship, the *SS Sunset*. Carrying 4,000 passengers and 1,500 crew, it was their flagship liner and on this special two-night media and VIP guests only maiden cruise from Southampton, nothing was going to spoil the launch.

The Ballater Battalion Bagpipe Band were playing along the quay and their music had drowned out the Captain's own drownings.

Rendez had no time to wait for the Captain. She had to interview the head bagpiper, Jock McSporran.

"You must be very proud, Jock, to lead such a procession of bagpipers?"

"Aye, lass, that I am."

Jock could see out of the corner of his eye the Captain steadying himself.

"Help ma boab whits happening over there?"

"Oh the Captain fell in the water after avoiding a Frenchman on a bicycle. Come to think of it, where did that cyclist go?"

"Och aye, the Captain looks droukit!"

"Sorry?"

"Wet lass, he's looking very wet."

The Captain and First Officer made their way into the *Sunset*.

The Captain went for a change of clothes while the First Officer welcomed passengers on board.

"Good afternoon, sir, madam, I'm First Officer Phil Offul."

"I certainly hope not, how dare you! I look very well for my age," said an elderly VIP passenger.

"He wasn't saying you looked awful, he was confirming his name is Offul!" whispered her husband.

It was going to be a long shift for the First Officer.

Part 3: Miss Fortune has no fortune with the media party.

With media guests, VIP passengers, crew and supplies safely on board, the *SS Sunset's* Sailaway was surprisingly silent down the Solent. A fracas of fireworks, however, ensured much noise and celebration behind her.

This maiden cruise gave ZNC the opportunity to showcase the *SS Sunset* to the media and her VIP passengers. A champagne reception had been organised and Captain Kibosh and Miss Fortune were in attendance. Rendez Vous was quick to interview Miss Fortune.

"You must be excited about the *SS Sunset* now that it's officially launched, Miss Fortune?"

"Oh yes, I am, and shortly we're going to introduce you to our new staff at the bar."

"I don't see anyone."

"Oh, they're not human, but robots, Mrs Vous. Very efficient and, of course, cheap."

Miss Fortune made her way over to the bar.

"Good evening, ladies and gentlemen, and welcome to this two-night maiden cruise of our new ship, the *SS Sunset*. The ship is brimming with the latest technology and I'd like to introduce our two newest recruits, 'Chip' and 'Pin'."

There was rapturous applause.

Chip and Pin were mechanical arms but something was wrong. Chip had spilt his drink and Pin threw his over Miss Fortune.

There was much laughter in the room. Miss Fortune was flapping.

"How do you turn them off?" she asked a colleague as she wiped away the drink.

"Has Pin slipped you a Gin, Miss Fortune?" asked a reporter.

"More champagne, now," demanded the Captain.

An Engineer was called to fix Chip and Pin immediately.

Part 4: The champers is shambolic. Mrs Vous is fortunate.

The *SS Sunset* arrived in Zeebrugge early morning and ZNC had a busy day. Stage two of Le Tour was arriving later in the afternoon and ZNC were co-sponsoring the event as well as presenting a prize to today's stage winner. A marquee would be beside the quayside which would host a media party. Miss Fortune was planning the day ahead with her assistant, Miss Lead.

"Go and check on our champagne supplies below, Miss Lead, and I'll meet you at our marquee."

Miss Lead went downstairs to the supply deck but an unpleasant surprise awaited her. A fellow crew member was slumped over a large crate.

"Give me a hand with this, will you?" she asked her colleague.

There was a slight groan. Miss Lead pushed him off the crate and opened it. There was nothing inside.

"Where is all our champagne?" she asked with a panic in her voice.

"We ran out last night, apart from this bottle," he said with a grin.

Miss Lead grabbed the bottle from her colleague. It was empty. Her colleague lay back down again.

Meanwhile, near the finishing line Mrs Vous was interviewing the Assistant Tour Director, Henri Wheel.

"Is it a difficult decision starting Le Tour outside of France?" she asked.

"Not at all, we like to expand its market. Remember the success of Yorkshire."

Mrs Vous suddenly noticed a cyclist hurtling towards them.

"It's a bit early for a stage winner now, isn't it?" she asked Henri.

"That cyclist isn't in the race!" he shouted to Rendez, nudging her out of the way. They were both held in each other's company for a few seconds. The cyclist sped off without stopping.

"Are you alright?" Henri asked.

"Yes, fine, thanks, but that's the second time in as many days a cyclist has tried to run me over."

"Have you not brought the champagne?" asked Miss Fortune as she saw Miss Lead approaching.

"We've run out," confirmed Miss Lead.

"OMG, how did that happen! What are we going to do now?"

"I think I saw a wine shop earlier, I could see if they have any?" asked Miss Lead.

Part 5: Le Tour's in town. Miss Lead is misled.

Miss Lead entered the local wine shop, looking to buy several bottles of champagne. She was met by the owner, Jean Le Cidre.

"How can I help you, madam?"

"I need as much champagne as you can give me."

Le Cidre spotted an opportunity.

Back at ZNC's marquee, the First Officer and Miss Fortune were in a group with Mrs Vous, Henri Wheel and Mr and Mrs Cruz-On, ZNC's only resident passengers.

"I believe your husband is racing in the Tour, Mrs Vous?" asked Phil Offul.

"Yes, he is."

"Does he have a chance of winning?"

"The whole Tour, no, but perhaps today's stage," Rendez replied with a smile.

"A bit of a sprinter then?" asked Mr Cruz-On.

"Oh yes, my husband De Ja Vous is very fast," confirmed Rendez.

A waiter offered some drinks. Miss Fortune looked aghast. Something was wrong. She headed towards Miss Lead.

"Why are we not serving champagne?" she asked her assistant.

"I thought we were?" Miss Lead replied.

They both walked over to the bar and found what Miss Lead had purchased.

"This isn't champagne, Miss Lead, but a cheap plonk! Tell me you didn't pay a lot for this?"

Miss Lead fell silent.

"No one will notice after a few drinks anyway," confirmed Mr Beer, the head barman. He winked to Miss Lead.

The moment was interrupted by the Captain, speaking on the tannoy.

"Ladies and gentlemen, the riders in the Tour will be arriving very shortly. Please make your way to the Grandstand near the finishing line where we have reserved seats."

Part 6: The Stage is set for a climactic ending, but not everyone is happy with the result.

There was a long straight to the finish line which gave the crowd there an excellent view. The sprinters were lining up at the front of the peloton and in an exciting finish, De Ja Vous managed the stage win by a tyre thread's lead as they went hurtling past the line to tumultuous applause.

Rendez gave out a loud screech of joy as she made her way across towards her husband. There was a frenzy of media around him.

"That was a very close finish, De Ja, did you use your team mate's slip-stream?" asked one of many reporters.

"Yes, it's always good to get behind someone else's wheel," De Ja replied.

"That's not the first time I've heard that, but not from Mr Vous," whispered another reporter.

Miss Fortune was preparing for the presentation but spent a moment with her boyfriend, Henri Wheel.

"You seem rather distant, Henri, is everything OK" she asked.

"Yes, I'm fine, I'll see you afterwards," he replied rather sheepishly.

At the presentation, De Ja was presented with the yellow jersey by Miss Fortune. They kissed each other cheek to cheek.

Meanwhile in the background there were raised voices.

"A reporter made reference to a wheel earlier which I didn't like the tone of," Henri said towards Rendez.

Just then, the cyclist from earlier appeared but on foot.

"Who are you?" asked Mrs Vous.

"Your worst nightmare, having an affair while married to my brother!"

The raised voices continued which could now be heard from the presentation.

"What is Henri doing arguing with Rendez and that other man?" asked Miss Fortune towards De Ja.

"I could say the same about Rendez," he replied.

Several of the press sniffing a scandal, rushed across to the commotion.

"Are you thinking what I'm thinking?" asked De Ja.

"I think so, fancy a drink?" Miss Fortune asked.

By now, they were almost alone. There was a large crowd gathering and much arguing behind the presentation area. De Ja Vous and Miss Fortune walked away almost unnoticed to a nearby café.

Lightning Source UK Ltd.
Milton Keynes UK
UKOW05f2344220217

295113UK00001B/173/P